Laura Valentine

Beautiful Bouquets

Culled from the poets of all countries

Laura Valentine

Beautiful Bouquets
Culled from the poets of all countries

ISBN/EAN: 9783337419356

Printed in Europe, USA, Canada, Australia, Japan

Cover: Foto ©Andreas Hilbeck / pixelio.de

More available books at **www.hansebooks.com**

BEAUTIFUL BOUQUETS,
CULLED FROM THE POETS OF ALL COUNTRIES.

THE

FORGET-ME-NOT.

𝔚𝔦𝔱𝔥 𝔊𝔬𝔩𝔬𝔲𝔯𝔢𝔡 𝔍𝔩𝔩𝔲𝔰𝔱𝔯𝔞𝔱𝔦𝔬𝔫𝔰

FROM ORIGINAL DESIGNS.

LONDON:
FREDERICK WARNE AND CO.
BEDFORD STREET, COVENT GARDEN.
NEW YORK: SCRIBNER, WELFORD AND CO.
1869.

LONDON:
SAVILL, EDWARDS AND CO., CHANDOS STREET,
COVENT GARDEN.

CONTENTS.

———

		PAGE
Recollections	Hon. Mrs. Norton	1
First Love's Recollections	John Clare	3
The Legend of the Forget-me-Not	Anonymous	4
From the German		9
Forget-me-Not	W. H. Harrison	10
The Bride of the Danube	Miss Pickersgill	15
In the Twilight Deep and Silent	Lowell	17
The Forsaken to the False One	Anon.	19
Think on Me	John Hamilton	21
" Forget-me-Not"		22
Eve	Hood	22
From the " Rape of Proserpine"	Barry Cornwall	23
Sensitive Plant	Mrs. Sigourney	24
Remembrance	Shakspeare	25

Contents.

		PAGE
Absence	Mrs. Butler (*née* Fanny Kemble)	26
I Think of Thee	Goethe	28
My Birthday	Thomas Moore	29
A Remembrance	Tennyson	31
Forget-me-Not	D. M. Moir	32
A Bouquet	Miss Landon, Mary Howitt	34
There are Moments in Life that are Never Forgot	Percival	34
Forget Thee?	Rev. John Moultrie	35
Remembrance	Thomas Hood	37
Good Night.	Miss Landon	38
The Wedding Wake	George Darley	39
Thekla's Song.	Schiller	41
May Song	Lord Thurlow	43
Sweet Morn!	Sterling	45
Toil	Elizabeth Barrett Browning	46
Do They Miss Me?	C. A. Briggs	47
The Pansy		49
The Country Child's Lantern	Clare	49
Narcissus and Violet	Miss Landon, Shelley	49
Stanzas for Music	Byron	50
The Friends that are Gone		52
Sonnet	Shakspeare	53
Alpine Gentian	Coleridge	53

Contents.

PAGE

Song . . . . Miss Landon   54

Common Ragwort 54

Flora's Garland 55

Lynaria—Yellow Toadflax 55

Foxglove 55

The Garden . . . . . "Hickes's Devotions"   56

Flowers . . . . Clare   58

To a Favourite Polyanthus . . . . . G. W.   59

Stanzas to Two Early Violets . . . . . Anon.   60

A Thought of the Daisy when in Brazil . Gardner   61

Love Shut Out of a Flower-Garden Roderigo Cotta   62

Sweet Peas . . . . Keats   64

On a Faded Violet . . . . Shelley   65

The First Morning of Spring . . . . Sigourney   66

Sonnet to the Camelia Japonica . . . W. Roscoe   67

Spring in New York . . . . . . Bryant   68

The Violet . . . . Anon.   71

Sonnet . . . . J. E. R.   72

The Knight and Lady Fair . . . Bishop Mant   73

Daffodils . . . . Wordsworth   75

Love's Bed of State . . . . Daniel   76

A Wee Flower . . . . Anderson   77

The Broken Flower . . . . Hemans   79

A Thought of the Rose . . . . . Mrs. Hemans   80

vi *Contents.*

                                                              PAGE

Heart's-Ease . . . . Mrs. Sheridan 81

Heart's-Ease . . . . Anon. 82

The Bee and the Lady Flower . . . . Herrick 83

Song of the Captive . . . . Goethe 85

The Almond Tree . . . . . . Miss Landon 89

Lines on Receiving a Branch of Mezereon Mrs. Tighe 91

Song 93

Summer Flowers . . . . . . Mrs. Hemans 94

The Blind Flower Girl's Song . . . . . Bulwer 95

Remembrance . . . . T. G. A. 97

Home . . . . Richard Hill 102

Song of the Forget-me-Not 103

Swiss Home-Sickness . . . . . Mrs. Hemans 104

As It Fell Upon a Day . . . . . Shakspeare 106

Philoctetes . . . . Wordsworth 108

The Lotus . . . . Tennyson 109

The Grecian Maidens Remember Sappho . Moore 111

The Shepherd of King Admetus . . . . Lowell 112

Sappho . . . . Croly 113

Cupid and Pysche . . . . . . T. K. Harvey 115

Cupid Carrying Provisions . . . . . Croly 117

The Origin of Fable . . . . Keats 119

Pilgrimage . . . . Miss Landon 122

A Truth . . . . Anonymous 123

PAGE

Thoughts on Flowers . . . . "The Casket" 124

Light in Darkness . . . . W. H. Burleigh 126

Self-Knowledge . . . . . . Sir John Davies 128

Floreal . . . . Kent, Wordsworth 129

Jeanie Morrison . . . . William Motherwell 131

Of a' the Airts the Wind can Blaw . . . Burns 135

May-Morn Song . . . . Motherwell 136

My Ain Countrie . . . . Allan Cunningham 138

Dinna Forget . . . . Anon. 139

The Auld Man . . . . Burns 140

Adieu for Evermore 141

Forget-me-Not 143

The Shepherd to the Flowers . . . . Raleigh 144

Sweet Day, so Cool . . . . . . G. Herbert 145

That Song again . . . . . . T. K. Harvey 146

Cupid and the Dial . . . . Anon. 147

"Servant to a Wooden Cradle" Julia W. Howe 148

Flowers . . . . Shelley 150

Remembrance . . . . . . Julia W. Howe 152

THE FORGET-ME-NOT.

RECOLLECTIONS.

DO you remember all the sunny places,
   Where, in bright days long past, we played
      together?
Do you remember all the old home faces
That gather'd round the hearth in wintry weather?
Do you remember all the happy meetings,
In summer evenings, round the open door—
Kind looks, kind hearts, kind words and tender greetings,
And clasping hands whose pulses beat no more?
               Do you remember them?

Do you remember all the merry laughter,
The voices round the swing in our old garden;
The dog that when we ran still follow'd after;
The teasing frolic sure of speedy pardon ?

3   B

We were but children then, young happy creatures,
And hardly knew how much we had to lose;
But now the dreamlike memory of those features
Comes back, and bids my darken'd spirit muse.
　　　　Do you remember them?

Do you remember when we first departed
From all the old companions who were round us,
How very soon again we grew light-hearted,
And talk'd with smiles of all the links which bound us?
And after, when our footsteps were returning,
With unfelt weariness, o'er hill and plain,
How our young hearts kept boiling up, and burning
To think how soon we'd be at home again?
　　　　Do you remember this?

Do you remember how the dreams of glory
Kept fading from us like a fairy treasure;
How we thought less of being famed in story,
And more of those to whom our fame gave pleasure?
Do you remember in far countries weeping,
When a light breeze, a flower, hath brought to mind
Old happy thoughts, which till that hour were sleeping,
And made us yearn for those we left behind?
　　　　Do you remember this?

Do you remember when no sound woke gladly,
But desolate echoes through our home were ringing,
How for a while we talk'd—then paused full sadly,
Because our voices bitter thoughts were bringing?

Ah me! those days—those days! My friend, my
    brother,
Sit down and let us talk of all our woe,
For we have nothing left but one another,—
Yet where they went, old playmate, we shall go ;
        Let us remember this.
                        Hon. Mrs. Norton.

—————◆—————

FIRST LOVE'S RECOLLECTIONS.

Oh, long be my heart with such memories filled!
Like the vase in which odours have once been distilled ;
You may break, you may ruin the vase, if you will,
But the scent of the roses will hang round it still !
                        Moore.

First love will with the heart remain,
    When its hopes are all gone by ;
As frail rose-blossoms still retain
    Their fragrance when they die.
And joy's first dreams will haunt the mind
    With the shades from which they sprung ;
As summer leaves the stems behind
    On which spring's blossoms hung
                        John Clare.

THE LEGEND OF THE FORGET-ME-NOT.

FAREWELL! my true and loyal knight! on
    yonder battle field
    Many a pearl and gem of price will gleam on
    helm and shield:
But bear thou on thy silver crest this pure and simple
    wreath,
A token of thy ladye's love—unchanging to the death.

They seem, I know, these fragrant flowers, those fairy
    stars of blue,
As maidens' eyes had smiled on them, and given them
    that bright hue ;
As only fitting but to bind a lady's hair or lute,
And not with war or warrior's crest in armed field to
    suit.

But there's a charm in every leaf, a deep and mystic
    spell ;
Then take the wreath, my loyal knight, our Lady shield
    thee well ;

And though still prouder favours deck the gallant
 knights of France,
Oh, be the first in every field, La Fleur de Souvenance !

How bland, how still this summer eve, sure never gentler
 hour
For lay of love, or sigh of lute, to breathe in lady's
 bower;
Then listen with a lover's faith, as spell-bound to the
 spot,
To the legend of my token flower, the charmed Forget-
 me-Not.

Young Albert led his Ida forth, when the departing sun
Still linger'd in the golden west, and shone like treasures
 won
From some far land of old romance; some genie's
 diamond throne,
A wreck of bright enchanted gems, in triumph over-
 thrown.

Love, look towards those radiant clouds, so like to fairy
 bowers:
How proudly o'er a sea of gold are raised their ruby
 towers ;
And now, as if by magic spell, a bright pavilion seems,
With its folds of sapphire light, where the panting sun-
 ray gleams.

To that bright heaven with smiles she looked ; one gleam
  of her blue eyes,
And Albert's heart forgot the clouds, and all their radiant
  dyes,
All, all, but that young smiling one, whose beauty well
  might seem
A fairy form of loveliness imagined in a dream.

She took a chaplet from her brow, which, gleaming soft
  and fair,
Like orient veil of amber light streamed down her silken
  hair,
Shedding fragrance and emitting brightness from its
  glittering rings,
As if hallow'd by Love's breath, and the glancing of his
  wings.

"These maiden roses, love, appear like pearls kissed
  by the sun
With last rich gleam of crimson ere his western throne
  be won ;
But should there not be some bright flower to deck our
  bridal wreath,
Whose hue might speak of constancy, unchanging to the
  death ?"

" My Ida ! from a thousand wreaths, thy own sweet
  fancy chose,
For pure unfading loveliness, this garland of the Rose :

And what can speak of truer faith, my own beloved one,
Than the flower whose fragrance lasts even when its life
is gone ? '

" Look to yon lone enchanted isle, which 'mid the
silvery foam
Of the blue water seems to float, the wild swan's elfin
home ;
A very cloud of azure flowers in rich profusion bloom ;
Winds of the lake ! your passing sighs breathe of their
rich perfume.

"In nameless beauty all unmarked, in solitude they
smile,
As if they bloomed but for the stars, or birds of that
lone isle :
For never yet hath mortal foot touched that enchanted
shore,
Long hallowed by the wildly imagined tales of yore.

" Full well I love those distant flowers, whose pure and
tender blue
Seems fitting emblem of a faith, unchanging as their
hue ;
And wouldst thou venture for my love as thou wouldst
for renown,
To win for me those azure flowers, to deck my bridal
crown ?"

One parting kiss of his fair bride, and swiftly far away,
Like the wild swan whose home he sought, young Albert
    met the spray
Of rising waves, which foamed in wrath, as if some
    spirit's hand
Awoke the genii of the lake to guard their mystic land.

The flowers were won, but devious his course lay back
    again;
To stem the waters in their tow'ring rage he strove in
    vain:
Fondly he glanced to the yet distant shore, where in
    despair
His Ida stood with outstretched arms, 'mid shrieks and
    tears and pray'r.

Darker and fiercer gathered on the tempest in its wrath,
The eddying waves with vengeful ire beset the fatal path;
With the wild energy of death he well-nigh reached the
    spot,
The azure flowers fell at her feet—" Ida, Forget me
    not!"
The words yet borne upon his lips, the prize seem'd
    almost won,
When 'mid the rush of angry waves he sank—for ever
    gone!

Within a proud cathedral aisle was raised a costly tomb,
Whose pure white marble like ethereal light amid the
    gloom

Shone—and no other trace it bore of lineage or of lot
But I!a's name, with star-like flowers ensculp'd Forget
    me not!

There Ida slept, the desolate, the last of all her name,
Parted from him who perished for her love 'mid dawn
    of fame;
But when shall their fond legend die! or when shall be
    forgot
The flower that won its name in death, Love's theme—
    Forget-me-Not?

ANONYMOUS.

FROM THE GERMAN.

SHEPHERDESS fair and dear!
How sweetly they buried thee here;
All the zephyrs mourned and sighed
And the blue-bells tolled when their lov'd one died,
Torches the glow-worm had borne by thy side,
If the stars had not beamed in their grief and pride;
Garments of sadness the sad night wore,
And the dark shadows bent them thy coffin o'er,
And the morning dews shall weep long and fast,
And the sun o'er thy grave shall his blessing cast.
Shepherdess fair and dear,
How sweetly they buried thee here!

FORGET ME NOT.

THE star that shines so pure and bright,
　　Like a far-off place of bliss,
　　And tells the broken-hearted
　　　　There are brighter worlds than this;
The moon that courses through the sky,
　　Like man's uncertain doom,
Now shining bright with borrowed light,
　　Now wrapp'd in deepest gloom,—
Or when eclips'd, a dreary blank,
　　A fearful emblem given
Of the heart shut out by a sinful world
　　From the blessed light of heaven;—
The flower that freely casts its wealth
　　Of perfume on the gale;
The breeze that mourns the summer's close,
　　With melancholy wail;
The stream that cleaves the mountain's side,
　　Or gurgles from the grot,—
All speak in their Creator's name,
　　And say "Forget me not!"

When man's vain heart is swollen with pride,
  And his haughty lip is curl'd,
And from the scorner's seat he smiles
  Contempt upon the world;
Where glitter crowns and coronets,
  Like stars that gem the skies,
And Flattery's incense rises thick
  To blind a monarch's eyes;
Where the courtier's tongue with facile lie
  A royal ear beguiles;
Where suitors live on promises,
  And sycophants on smiles;
Where each as in a theatre
  Is made to play his part,
Where the diadem hides a troubled brow,
  And the star an aching heart;
There, even 'mid pomp and power,
  Is oft a voice that calls
" Forget me not," in thunder,
  Throughout the palace walls.

Or in the house of banqueting,
  Where the madd'ning bowl is flush,
And the shameless ribald boast of deeds
  For which the cheek should blush;
Where from the oft-drain'd goblet's brim
  The eye of mirth is lit;
Where the cold conceits of a trifler's brain
  Pass for the coin of wit;

Where Flattery sues to woman's ear,
 And tells his tale again,
And Beauty smiles upon things so mean,
 We blush to call them men;
Where 'tis sad to hear the flippant tongue
 Apply its hackneyed arts;—
Oh! their heads would be the hollowest things.
 But for their hollower hearts!
But, hist! the reveller's shout is still'd,
 The song, the jest forgot;
The hair is snapp'd, the sword descends,
 With a dread " Forget me not!"

Go! hie thee to the rank churchyard
 Where flits the shadowy ghost,
And see how little pride has left
 Whereon to raise a boast.
See Beauty claiming sisterhood
 With the noisome reptile worm—
Oh, where are all the graces fled
 That once array'd her form!
Fond hope no more on her smile will feed,
 Nor wither at her frown:
Her head will rest more quiet now
 Than when it slept on down.
With cloven crest and bloody shroud
 The once proud warrior lies;
And the patriot's heart hath not a throb
 To give to a nation's cries.

A solemn voice will greet thine ear
  As thou lingerest round the spot,
And cry from out the sepulchre,
  " Frail man, forget me not !"

" Forget me not !" the thunder roars,
  As it bursts its sulphury cloud ;
'Tis murmur'd by the distant hills
  In echoes long and loud ;
'Tis written by the Almighty's hand
  In characters of flame,
When the lightnings gleam with vivid flash,
  And His wrath and power proclaim.
'Tis murmur'd when the white wave falls
  Upon the wreck-strewn shore,
As a hoary warrior bows his crest
  When his day of work is o'er.
Go ! speed thee forth when the beamy sun
  O'erthrows the reign of night,
And strips the scene of its misty robe,
  And arrays it in diamonds bright.
Oh ! as thou drinkest health and joy
  In the fresh and balmy air,
" Forget me not," in a still small voice
  Will surely greet thee there.

Oh ! who that sees the vermeil cheek
  Grow day by day more pale,
And Beauty's form to shrink before
  The summer's gentlest gale,

But thinks of Him, the mighty One,
  By whom the blow is given,
As if the fairest flowers of earth
  Were early pluck'd for heaven.
Oh! yes, on every side we see
  The impress of His hand;
The air we breathe is full of Him,
  And the earth on which we stand
Yet heedless man regards it not,
  But life's uncertain day
In idle hopes and vain regrets
  Thus madly wastes away.
But in his own appointed time
  He will not be forgot :
Oh! in that hour of fearful strife,
  Great God, forget me not !

                    W. H. HARRISON.

THE BRIDE OF THE DANUBE.

SEE how yon glittering wave in sportive play,
Washes the bank, and steals the flowers away.
And must they thus in bloom and beauty die,
Without the passing tribute of a sigh?

" No, Bertha, those young flow'rets there
Shall form a braid for thy sunny hair;
I yet will save them, if but one
Soft smile reward me when 'tis done."
He said, and plung'd into the stream—
His only light was the moon's pale beam.
" Stay! stay!" She cried—but he had caught
The drooping flow'rs, and breathless sought
To place the treasures at the feet
Of her from whom e'en death were sweet.

With outstretch'd arms upon the shore she stood,
With tearful eye she gaz'd upon the flood,
Whose swelling tide now seem'd as if 'twould sever
Her faithful lover from her arms for ever.
Still through the surge he panting strove to gain
The welcome strand—but, ah! he strove in vain!

Yet once the false stream bore him to the spot
Where stood his bride in muteness of despair;
And scarcely had he said, "Forget me not!"
And flung the dearly ransom'd flow'rets there,
When the dark wave clos'd o'er him, and no more,
Was seen young Rodolph on the Danube's shore.

Aghast she stood; she saw the tranquil stream
Pass o'er him—could it be a fleeting dream?
Ah, no! the last fond words, "Forget me not!"
Told it was all a sad reality.
With frantic grasp the dripping flow'rs she prest,
Too dearly purchas'd, to her aching breast.

Alas! her tears, her sorrows now were vain,
For him she lov'd she ne'er shall see again!
Is this then a bridal, where, sad in her bow'r,
The maid weeps alone at the nuptial hour;
Where hush'd is the harp, and silent the lute—
Ah! why should their thrilling strains be mute?
And where is young Rodolph? where stays the bride-
    groom?
Go, ask the dark waters, for there is his tomb.

Often at eve when maidens rove
Beside the Danube's wave,
They tell the tale of hapless love,
And show young Rodolph's grave;
And cull the flowers from that sweet spot,
Still calling them "Forget-me-Not."

                                    Miss Pickersgill.

IN THE TWILIGHT DEEP AND SILENT.

IN the twilight deep and silent
   Comes thy spirit unto mine;
When the starlight and the moonlight
   Over cliff and woodland shine,
And the quiver of the river
   Seems a thrill of joy benign.

Then I rise and go in fancy
   To the headland by the sea;
When the evening star throbs setting
   Through the dusky cedar tree,
And, from under, low-voiced thunder
   From the surf swells fitfully.

Then within my soul I feel thee
   Like a dream of bygone years:
Visions of my childhood murmur
   Their old madness in my ears,
Till the pleasance of thy presence
   Crowds my heart with blissful tears.

*   *   *   *   *

All the wondrous dreams of boyhood,
  All youth's fiery thirst of praise,
All the surer hopes of manhood,
  Blossoming in sadder days,—
Joys that bound me, griefs that crowned me,
  With a better wreath than bays,—

All the longings after freedom,
  The vague love of human-kind—
Wandering far and near at random,
  Like a dead leaf on the wind,
Rousing only in the lonely
  Twilight of an aimless mind—

All of these, oh, best-beloved!
  Happiest present dreams and past,
In thy love find safe fulfilment
  Ripened into truth at last;
Faith and beauty, hope and duty,
  To one centre gather fast.

How my spirit, like an ocean,
  At the breath of thine awakes,
Leaps its shores in mad exulting,
  And in foamy music breaks;
Then, down-sinking, lieth shrinking
  From the tumult that it makes.

                              LOWELL.

THE FORSAKEN TO THE FALSE ONE.

DARE thee to forget me! go, wander where
thou wilt!
Thy hand upon the vessel's helm, or on the
sabre's hilt.
Away! thou'rt free—o'er land and sea, go rush to danger's
brink:
But oh, thou can'st not fly from thought—thy curse shall
be to think.

Remember me! remember all my long-enduring love,
Which linked itself to perfidy—the vulture and the dove:
Remember in thy utmost need I never once did shrink,
But clung to thee confidingly—thy curse shall be to think.

Then go! that thought will render thee a dastard in the
fight,
That thought when thou art tempest-toss'd will fill thee
with affright;
In some vile dungeon may'st thou lie, and, counting each
cold link,
That binds thee to captivity,—thy curse shall be to think.

Go! seek the merry banquet-hall where younger maidens
    bloom,
The thought of me shall make thee there endure a
    deeper gloom;
That thought will turn the festive cup to poison while
    you drink,
And while false smiles are on thy cheek—thy curse shall
    be to think.

Forget me! false one! hope it not,—when minstrels
    touch the string,
The memory of other days will gall thee while they
    sing;
The air I used to love will make thy coward conscience
    shrink,
Ay! every note will have its sting—thy curse shall be
    to think.

ANON.

THINK ON ME.

GO where the water glideth gently ever—
　　Glideth through meadows that the greenest be,
Go, listen to our own beloved river,
　　　　And think on me.

Wander in forests where the small flower layeth
Her fancy gem beneath the giant tree;
List to the dim brook, pining as it playeth,
　　　　And think on me.

And when the sky is silver pale at even,
And the wind grieveth in the lonely tree:
Walk out beneath the solitary heaven,
　　　　And think on me.

And when the moon riseth as she were dreaming,
And treadeth with white feet the lulled sea,
Go, silent as a star beneath her beaming,
　　　　And think on me.

　　　　　　　　　JOHN HAMILTON.

The Forget-me-Not.

" FORGET-ME-NOT."

THERE is a little modest flower,
　　To friendship ever dear,
'Tis nourished in her humble bower,
　　And watered by her tear.

If hearts by fond affection tried,
　　Should chance to slip away,
This little flower will gently chide
　　The heart that thus would stray.

All other flowers when once they fade
　　Are left alone to die,
But this, e'en when it is decayed,
　　Will live in memory's sigh.

EVE.

WHERE are the blooms of summer?—In the West,
Blushing their last to the last sunny hours,
When the mild eve by sudden night is prest,
Like tearful Proserpine, snatch'd from her flowers
To a most gloomy breast.

　　　　　　　　　　　　HOOD.

FROM THE "RAPE OF PROSERPINE."

HERE, this rose
(This one half-blown) shall be my Maia's portion,
For that like it her blush is beautiful;
And this deep violet, almost as blue
As Pallas' eye, or thine Lycinnia,
I'll give to thee; for like thyself it wears
Its sweetness, ne'er obtruding.   For this lily,
Where can it hang but at Cyane's breast?
And yet 'twill wither on so white a bed,
If flowers have sense for envy :—It shall lie
Amongst thy raven tresses, Cytheris,
Like one star on the bosom of the night.
The cowslip, and the yellow primrose,—they
Are gone, my sad Leontia, to their graves,
And April hath wept o'er them, and the voice
Of March hath sung, even before their deaths,
The dirge of those young children of the year.
But here is heart's-ease for your woes.   And now,
The honey-suckle flower I give to thee,
And love it for my sake, my own Cyane:
It hangs upon the stem it loves, as thou
Hast clung to me, thro' every joy and sorrow;
It flourishes with its guardian's growth, as thou dost;
And if the woodman's axe should drop the tree,
The woodbine too must perish.
                              BARRY CORNWALL.

SENSITIVE PLANT

HERE is a plant that in its cell
　　All trembling seems to stand,
And　ends its stalk and folds its leaves
　　From each approaching hand

And thus there is a conscious nerve
　　Within the human breast,
That from the rash and careless hand
　　Shrinks, and retires distrest.

The pressure rude, the touch severe,
　　Will raise within the mind
A nameless thrill, a secret tear,
　　A torture undefined.

O you who are by nature form'd
　　Each thought refined to know,
Repress the word—the glance—that wakes
　　That trembling nerve to woe.

And be it still your joy to raise
  The trembler from the shade,
To bind the broken, and to heal
  The wound you never made.

Whene'er you see the feeling mind,
  Oh let this care begin !
And though the cell be e'er so low,
  Respect the guest within !

Mrs. Sigourney.

REMEMBRANCE.

When to the sessions of sweet silent thought
  I summon up remembrance of things past,
I sigh the lack of many a thing I sought,
  And with old woes new wail my dear time's waste;
Then can I drown an eye unused to flow,
  For precious friends hid in death's dateless night,
And weep afresh love's long-since cancelled woe,
  And moan the expense of many a vanished sight.
Then can I grieve at grievances forgone,
  And heavily from woe to woe tell o'er
The sad account of fore-bemoanèd moan,
  Which I now pay as if not paid before !
—But if the while I think on thee, dear friend,
All losses are restored, and sorrows end.

Shakspeare.

ABSENCE.

WHAT shall I do with all the days and hours
    That must be counted ere I see thy face?
How shall I charm the interval that lowrs
    Between this time and that sweet time of grace

Shall I in slumber steep each weary sense,
    Weary with longing? Shall I flee away
Into past days, and with some fond pretence
    Cheat myself to forget the present day?

Shall love for thee lay on my soul the sin
    Of casting from me God's great gift of time?
Shall I, these mists of memory lock'd within,
    Leave and forget life's purposes sublime!

Oh! how, or by what means, may I contrive
    To bring the hour that brings thee back more near?
How may I teach my drooping hope to live
    Until that blessed time, and thou art here?

I'll tell thee: for thy sake I will lay hold
  Of all good aims, and consecrate to thee,
In worthy deeds, each moment that is told,
  While thou, beloved one ! art far from me.

For thee, I will arouse my thoughts to try
  All heavenward flights, all high and holy strains ;
For thy dear sake I will walk patiently
  Thro' these long hours, nor call their minutes pains.

I will this dreary blank of absence make
  A noble task time, and will therein strive
To follow excellence, and to o'ertake
  More good than I have won, since yet I live.

So may this doomèd time build up in me
  A thousand graces which shall thus be thine;
So may my love and longing hallowed be,
  And thy dear thought an influence divine.

MRS. BUTLER
(*née* FANNY KEMBLE).

I THINK OF THEE.

THINK of thee whene'er the sun is glowing
    Upon the lake ;
Of thee when in the crystal fountain flowing
    The moonbeams shake.

I see thee when the wanton wind is busy
    And dust-clouds rise ;
In the deep night, when o'er the bridge so dizzy
    The wanderer hies.

I hear thee when the waves, with hollow roaring,
    Gush forth their fill;
Often along the heath I go exploring
    When all is still.

I am with thee, though far thou art and darkling,
    Yet thou art near;
The sun goes down—the stars will soon be sparkling ;
    Oh, wert thou here !

GÖTHE.

MY BIRTHDAY.

" **M**Y birthday"—what a different sound
  That word had in my youthful years!
  And how, each time the day comes round,
  Less and less white the mark appears.
When first our scanty years are told,
It seems like pastime to grow old;
And, as youth counts the shining links
  That time around him binds so fast,
Pleased with the task, he little thinks
  How hard that chain will press at last.
Vain was the man, and false as vain,
  Who said—" Were he ordain'd to run
His long career of life again,
  He would do all that he had done."
Ah, 'tis not thus the voice that dwells
  In sober birthdays, speaks to me;
Far otherwise—of time it tells,
  Lavish'd unwisely—carelessly;
Of counsel mock'd, of talents, made
  Haply for high and pure designs,
But oft, like Israel's incense, laid
  Upon unholy, earthly shrines;

Of nursing many a wrong desire,
    Of wandering after love too far,
And taking every meteor fire
    That cross'd my pathway for his star !
All this it tells, and, could I trace
    The imperfect picture o'er again,
With power to add, re-touch, efface
    The lights and shades, the joy and pain,
How little of the past would stay !
How quickly all should melt away :
All but that freedom of the mind,
    Which hath been more than wealth to me ;
Those friendships, in my boyhood twined,
    And kept till now unchangingly ;
And that dear home, that saving ark,
    Where love's true light at last I've found,
Cheering within, when all grows dark,
    And comfortless, and stormy, round !

THOMAS MOORE.

A REMEMBRANCE.

REMEMBER you the clear moonlight
  That whitened all the eastern ridge,
  When o'er the water dancing white
I stepp'd upon the old mill bridge?
I heard you whisper from above,
A lute-toned whisper, I am here!
I murmur'd, speak again, my love,
The stream is loud: I cannot hear!

I heard, as I have seem'd to hear
When all the under air was still,
The low voice of the glad new year
Call to the freshly-flower'd hill.
I heard, as I have often heard,
The nightingale in leafy woods
Call to its mate when nothing stirr'd
To left or right, but falling floods!

TENNYSON.

FORGET ME NOT.

SUMMER was on the hills when last we parted.
   Now the bright moon is shining
      O'er the gray mountains and the stilly sea,
As, by the streamlet's willowy bend reclining,
  I pause, remembering thee.

Yes! as we roam'd, the sylvan earth seem'd glowing
  With many a beauty, unremark'd before;
The soul was like a deep urn overflowing
  With thoughts, a treasured store;
The very flowers seemed born but to exhale,
As breathed the west, their fragrance to the gale.

Methinks, even yet I feel thy timid fingers
  With their bland pressure thrilling bliss to mine;
Methinks, yet on my cheek thy breathing lingers
  As—fondly leant to thine,
I told, how life all pleasureless would be,
Green palm-tree of life's desert! wanting thee.

Not yet, not yet had disappointment shrouded
   Youth's summer calm with storms of wintry strife;
The star of hope shone o'er our path unclouded,
   And Fancy coloured life
With those elysian rainbow hues, which Truth
Melts with his rod, when disenchanting youth.

Yet should it cheer me, that nor Woe hath shattered
   The ties that link our hearts, nor Hate nor Wrath;
And soon the day may dawn, when shall be scattered
   All shadows from our path.
For ah! with others wealth and mirth would be
Less sweet, by far, than sorrow shared with thee!

Yes! vainly, foolishly the vulgar reckon,
   That happiness resides in outward shows:
Contentment from the lowliest cot may beckon
   True Love to sweet repose:
For genuine bliss can ne'er be far apart,
When soul meets soul, and heart respor ds to heart.

D. M. MOIR.

A BOUQUET.

THE tulip
Whose passionate leaves with their ruby glow
Hide the breast that is burning and black below.

MISS LANDON.

THE almond, though its branch is sere,
With myriad blossoms beautiful,
As pink as is the shell's inside.

MARY HOWITT.

———◆———

THERE ARE MOMENTS IN LIFE THAT ARE NEVER FORGOT.

THERE are moments in life that are never forgot,
  Which brighten and brighten as time steals away;
They give a new charm to the happiest lot,
  And they shine on the gloom of the loneliest day.

These moments are hallow'd by smiles, and by tears—
  The first look of love, and the last parting given;
As the sun in the dawn of his glory appears,
  And the cloud weeps and glows with the rainbow in
    heaven.

PERCIVAL.

FORGET THEE?

" ORGET thee?"—If to dream by night, and
    muse on thee by day;
    If all the worship, deep and wild, a poet's
    heart can pay,
If prayers in absence, breathed for thee to Heaven's pro-
    tecting power,
If wingèd thoughts that flit to thee a thousand in an
    hour,
If busy Fancy, blending thee with all my future lot,—
If this thou call'st "forgetting," thou indeed shalt be
    forgot !

" Forget thee?"—Bid the forest birds forget their sweetest
    tune !
" Forget thee?"—Bid the sea forget to swell beneath the
    moon ;
Bid the thirsty flowers forget to drink the eve's refreshing
    dew ;
Thyself forget thine "own dear land," and its "moun-
    tains wild and blue ;"

Forget each old familiar face, each long-remember'd spot :
When these things are forgot by thee, then thou shalt be
    forgot !

Keep, if thou wilt, thy maiden peace, still calm and
    fancy-free ;
For God forbid thy gladsome heart should grow less
    glad for me !
Yet, while that heart is still unwon, oh, bid not mine to
    rove,
But let it keep its humble faith, and uncomplaining love ;
If these, preserved for patient years, at last avail me not,
Forget me then ;—but ne'er believe that thou canst be
    forgot !

Rev. John Moultrie.

REMEMBRANCE.

REMEMBER, I remember
The house where I was born,
The little window where the sun
Came peeping in at morn;
He never came a wink too soon
Nor brought too long a day ;
But now I often wish the night
Had borne my breath away !

I remember, I remember
The roses, red and white,
The violets, and the lily cups—
Those flowers made of light;
The lilacs, where the robins built,
And where my brother set
The laburnum on his birth-day,—
The tree is living yet !

I remember, I remember
The fir trees dark and high ;
I used to think their slender spires
Were close against the sky !
It was a childish ignorance,
But now 'tis little joy
To know I'm further off from heaven,
Than when I was a boy !

THOMAS HOOD.

GOOD NIGHT.

GOOD night!—what a sudden shadow
Has fallen upon the air,
I look not around the chamber,
I know he is not there.
Sweetness has left the music,
And gladness left the light,
My cheek has lost its colour,—
How could he say good night!
And why should he take with him
The happiness he brought?
Alas! such fleeting pleasure
Is all too dearly bought,
If thus my heart stop beating,
My spirits lose their tone,
And a gloom like night surrounds me,
The moment he is gone.
Like the false fruit of the lotos,
Love alters every taste,
We loathe the life we are leading,
The spot where we are placed;
We live upon to-morrow,
Or we dream the past again,
But what avails that knowledge,
It ever comes in vain.

MISS LANDON.

THE WEDDING WAKE.

WE'LL carry her o'er the churchyard green,
  Down by the willow trees ;
We'll bury her by herself between
  The sister cypresses.

Flowers of the sweetest, saddest hue,
  Shall deck her lowly bed,
Rosemary at her feet we'll strew,
  And violets at her head.

The pale rose, the dim azure bell,
  And that lamenting flower,
With ai ! ai ! its eternal knell,
  Shall overbloom her bower,—

Her cypress bower ; whose shade beneath
  Passionless she shall lie ;—
To rest so calm, so sweet in death,
  'Twere no great ill to die !

Ye four fair maids, the fairest ye,
   Be ye the flower-strewers!
Ye four bright youths the bearers be,
   Ye were her fondest wooers!

To church! to church! ungallant youth,
   Carry your willing bride!
So pale he looks! 'twere well, in sooth,
   He should lie by her side.

The bed is laid, the toll is done,
   The ready priest doth stand;
Come, let the flowers be strewn, be strewn,
   Strike up the bridal band.

GEORGE DARLEY.

THEKLA'S SONG.

[This song is said to have been composed by Schiller in answer to the inquiries of his friends respecting the fate of Thekla, whose beautiful character is withdrawn from the tragedy of "Wallenstein's Death," after her resolution to visit the grave of her lover is made known.]

ASK'ST thou my home?—my pathway wouldst
    thou know,
    When from thine eye my floating shadow
    pass'd?
Was not my work fulfill'd, and closed below?
  Had I not lived and loved?—my lot was cast.

Wilt thou ask where the nightingale is gone,
  That, melting into song her soul away,
Gave the spring breeze what witch'd thee in its tone?—
  But while she loved, she lived in that sad lay.

Think'st thou my heart its lost one hath not found?
  Yes! we are one; oh! trust me, we have met,—
Where nought again may part what Love hath bound,
  Where falls no tear, and whispers no regret.

There shalt thou find us—there with us be bless'd,
  If, as our love, thy love is pure and true;
There dwells my father,* sinless and at rest,
  Where the fierce murderer may no more pursue.

And well he feels, no error of the dust
  Drew to the stars of heaven his upward ken;
There it is with us, e'en as is our trust,
  He that believes, is near the Holy then.

There shall each feeling, beautiful and high,
  Keep the sweet promise of its earthly day—
Oh! fear thou not to dream with waking eye,
  There lies deep meaning oft in childish play.

* Wallenstein.

MAY SONG.

MAY, queen of blossoms,
  And fulfilling flowers,
With what pretty music
  Shall we charm the hours?
Wilt thou have pipe and reed,
Blown in the open mead?
Or to the lute give heed,
  In the green bowers?

Thou hast no need of us,
  Or pipe or wire,
That hast the golden bee
  Ripen'd with fire;
And many thousand more
Songsters, that thee adore,
Filling earth's grassy floor
  With new desire.

Thou hast thy mighty herds,
  Tame and free livers,

Doubt not, thy music too
  In the deep rivers,
And the whole plumy flight,
Warbling the day and night,—
Up at the gates of light,
  See, the lark quivers !

When with the jacinth
  Coy fountains are tress'd,
And for the mournful bird,
  Green woods are dress'd
That did for Tereus pine,
Then shall our songs be thine,
To whom our hearts incline,—
  May, be thou bless'd !

LORD THURLOW.

SWEET MORN!

SWEET morn! from endless cups of gold
    Thou liftest reverently on high
More incense fine than earth can hold,
    To fill the sky.

One interfusion wide of love,
    Thine airs and odours moist ascend,
And 'mid the azure depths above
    With light they blend,

And from the mountain ridges beam
    Above their quiet steeps of gray ;
The eastern clouds with glory stream
    And vital day.

A joy from hidden paradise
    Is rippling down the shiny brooks
With beauty, like the gleams of eyes
    In tenderest looks.

   *   *   *   *   *

In man, O morn ! a loftier good
   With conscious blessing fills the soul,
A life, by reason understood,
   Which metes the whole.

With healthful pulse and tranquil fire,
   Which plays at ease in every limb,
His thoughts unchecked to heaven aspire—
   Revealed in him.

STERLING.

TOIL.

WHAT are we set on earth for ?   Say to toil !
   Nor seek to leave thy tending of the vines
   For all the heat o' the day, till it declines
And Death's wild curfew shall from work assoil.
God did anoint thee with His odorous oil
   To wrestle, not to reign ; and He assigns
   All thy tears over like pure crystallines,
For younger fellow-workers of the soil
   To wear for amulets.   So others shall
Take patience, labour, to their heart and hand,
   From thy heart and thy hand and thy brave cheer;
   And God's grace fructify to thee through all.
The least flower with a brimming cup may stand
   And share its dew-drop with another near.

ELIZABETH BARRETT BROWNING.

DO THEY MISS ME?

DO they miss me at home, do they miss me?
    'Twould be an assurance most dear,
To know that this moment some loved one
    Was saying, " Oh, were she but here !"
To know that the group at the fireside
    Were thinking of me as I roam,—
Oh yes, 'twould be joy beyond measure,
    To *know* that they missed me at home!

When twilight approaches—the season
    That ever was sacred to song—
Does some one repeat my name over,
    And sigh that I tarry so long?
And is there a chord in the music
    That's missed when my voice is away ?
And a chord in each heart that awaketh
    Regret at my wearisome stay?

Do they place me a chair near the table
    When evening's home pleasures are nigh,

And candles are lit in the parlour,
    And stars in the calm azure sky ?
And when the good-nights are repeated,
    Does each the dear memory keep,
And think of the absent, and waft me
    A whispered " good-night " ere they sleep ?

Do they miss me at home, do they miss me,
    At morning, at noon, and at night ?—
And lingers one gloomy shade round them
    That only my presence can light ?—
Are joys less invitingly welcomed,
    And pleasures less dear than before,
Because one is missed from the circle—
    Because *I* am with them no more?

Oh yes—they do miss me—kind voices
    Are calling me back as I roam,
And eyes have grown weary with weeping,
    And watch but to welcome me home !
Sweet friends, ye shall wait me no longer,
    No longer I'll tarry behind—
For how can I tarry while followed
    By watchings and pleadings so kind ?

                              C. A. BRIGGS.

THE PANSY.

FRAGRANT the Pansy breathing from the meadows,
  As the west wind bows down the long green grass ;
Now dark, now golden, as the fleeting shadows
  Of the light clouds pass, as they wont to pass
      A long while ago.

————◆————

THE COUNTRY CHILD'S LANTERN.

A GLOWWORM found in lanes remote
Is murdered for its shining coat,
And put in flowers that nature weaves
With hollow shapes and silken leaves,—
Such as the Canterbury Bell,—
Serving for lamp or lantern well.

CLARE.

————◆————

NARCISSUS AND VIOLET.

THE pale and delicate narcissus' flowers
Bending so languidly, as still they found
In the pure wave a love and destiny.

MISS LANDON.

THE violet's azure eye
Which gazes on the sky
Until its hue grows like what it beholds.

SHELLEY.

3   E

STANZAS FOR MUSIC.

THERE'S not a joy the world can give like that it takes away,
    When the glow of early thought declines in feeling's dull decay;
'Tis not on youth's smooth cheek the blush alone, which fades so fast,
But the tender bloom of heart is gone, ere youth itself be past.

Then the few whose spirits float above the wreck of happiness
Are driven o'er the shoals of guilt or ocean of excess:
The magnet of their course is gone, or only points in vain
The shore to which their shiver'd sail shall never stretch again.

Then the mortal coldness of the soul like death itself comes down;
It cannot feel for others' woes, it dare not dream its own:

That heavy chill has frozen o'er the fountain of our
    tears,
And though the eye may sparkle still, 'tis where the ice
    appears.

Though wit may flash from fluent lips, and mirth dis-
    tract the breast,
Through midnight hours that yield no more their former
    hope of rest:
'Tis but as ivy-leaves around the ruin'd turret wreath,
All green and wildly fresh without, but worn and gray
    beneath.

Oh! could I feel as I have felt, or be what I have been,
Or weep as I could once have wept, o'er many a vanish'd
    scene ;
As springs in deserts found seem sweet, all brackish
    though they be,
So midst the wither'd waste of life those tears would
    flow to me.

                             BYRON.

THE FRIENDS THAT ARE GONE.

 O ye think of the hopes that are gone, Jeanie,
 As ye sit by your fire at night ?
Do ye gather them up as they faded fast
 Like buds with an early blight?"
"I think of the hopes that are gone, Robin,
 And I mourn not their stay was fleet ;
For they fell as the leaves of the red rose fall,
 And were even in falling sweet."

" Do ye think of the friends that are gone, Jeanie,
 As ye sit by your fire at night ?
Do ye wish they were round you again once more,
 By the hearth that they made so bright ?"
"I think of the friends that are gone, Robin,
 They are dear to my heart as then :
But the best and the dearest among them all
 I have never wished back again !"

SONNET.

THE forward violet thus did I chide:
 Sweet thief, whence didst thou steal thy sweet that
  smells,
If not from my love's breath? The purple pride
 Which on thy soft cheek for complexion dwells
In my love's veins thou hast too grossly dyed.
 The lily I condemned for thy hand,
And buds of marjoram had stolen thy hair:
 The roses fearfully on thorns did stand,
One blushing shame, another white despair:
 A third, nor red nor white, had stolen of both,
And to his robbery had annex'd thy breath;
 But, for his theft, in pride of all his growth
A vengeful canker eat him up to death,
More flowers I noted, yet I none could see,
But sweet or colour it had stolen from thee.

SHAKSPEARE.

ALPINE GENTIAN.

WHO, with living flowers
Of loveliest blue, spread garlands at your feet?
GOD! let the torrents, like a shout of nations,
Answer! And let the ice-plains echo GOD.

COLERIDGE.

SONG.

WAVE—that wanderest singing by,
  Bearing leaves and flowers with thee
To the lady of my heart
  Waft a benison from me.

Wind—that rov'st around the grove,
  Kissing every flower nigh,
I'll send thee on a sweeter search,
  Bear my own sweet love my sigh.

Tree—that show'st my graven word,
  Thine be yet a happier lot,
Mayst thou meet my maiden's eye,
  Bidding her " Forget me not."

MISS LANDON.

COMMON RAGWORT.

MY childhood's earliest thoughts are link'd with thee;
  The sight of thee calls back the robin's songs
Who from the dark old tree
  Beside the door, sang clearly all day long,
And I secure in childish piety,
  Listened as if I heard an angel sing,
With news from heaven, which he did bring
  Fresh every day to my untainted ears
  When birds and flowers and I were happy peers.

FLORA'S GARLAND.

Wreathed of the sunny Celandine—the brief
Courageous wind-flower, loveliest of the frail,—
The Hazel's crimson star,—the Woodbine's leaf,—
The Daisy with its half-closed eye of grief,
Prophets of fragrance, beauty, joy, and song.

———◆———

LINARIA—YELLOW TOADFLAX.

And thou, Linaria, mingle in my wreath
Thy golden dragons, for though perfumed breath
Escapes not from thy yellow petals, yet
Glad thoughts bringest thou of hedgerow foliage, wet
With tears and dew; lark warbling, and green ferns
O'er-spanning crystal runnels, where there turns
And twines the glossy ivy.

———◆———

FOXGLOVE.

Upon the sunny bank
The foxglove rears its pyramid of bells,
Gloriously freckled, purpled and white, the flower
That cheers Devonia's fields.

THE GARDEN.

HEN, dearest Lord, when shall I be
A garden seal'd to all but Thee?
No more expos'd, no more undone;
But live, and grow to Thee alone?

'Tis not, alas! on this low earth
That such pure flowers can find a birth
Only they spring above the skies,
Where none can live till here he dies.

Then let me die, that I may go,
And dwell where those bright lilies grow;
Where those best plants of glory rise,
And make a safer paradise.

No dangerous fruit, no tempting Eve,
No crafty serpent to deceive;
But we like gods indeed shall be;—
Oh! let me die that life to see.

Thus says my song: but does my heart
Join with the words, and sing its part?
Am I so thorough wise to choose
The other world, and this refuse?

Why should I not? What do I find
That fully here contents my mind?
What is this meat, and drink, and sleep,
That such poor things from heaven should keep?

What is this honour, or great place,
Or bag of money, or fair face?
What's all the world, that thus we should
Still long to dwell with flesh and blood?

Fear not, my soul, stand to thy word,
Which thou hast sung to thy dear Lord;
Let but thy love be firm and true,
And with more heat thy wish renew.

Oh may this dying life make haste
To die into true life at last;
No hope have I to live before,
But then to live and die no more.

Great, ever-living God, to Thee,
In essence one, in Persons three;
May all thy works their tribute bring,
And every age thy glory sing.
                    Amen.
            "HICKES'S DEVOTIONS."

FLOWERS.

BOWING adorers of the gale,
Ye cowslips delicately pale,
   Upraise your loaded stems;
Unfold your cups in splendour, speak!
Who decked you with that ruddy streak,
   And gilt your golden gems?

Violets, sweet tenants of the shade,
In purple's richest pride arrayed,
   Your errand here fulfil;
Go, bid the artist's simple strain
Your lustre imitate in vain,
   And match your Maker's skill.

Daisies, ye flowers of lowly birth,
Embroiderers of the carpet earth,
   That stud the velvet sod;
Open to Spring's refreshing air,
In sweetest smiling bloom declare
   Your Maker and my God.

CLARE.

TO A FAVOURITE POLYANTHUS.

HOW the rich cups of that so lovely flower
　　Lift to the heavens their purple velvet leaves !
　　That every petal, freshened by the shower
Which falls in dew-drops from its slanting eaves,
May feel the warm sap through its vessels run,
In glad obedience to the glowing sun.

Each fragrant chalice breathes upon the air
　　A scent more sweet than censer ever flung
In clouds of incense, blinding all the glare
　　Of garish candles, when the mass was sung :
"The long-drawn aisle," and the cathedral's gloom,
Ne'er felt the richness of such rare perfume.

With forms more graceful, and with vestments clad,
　　Such as the haughty prelate never wore,
They give to God an adoration glad,
　　That well might teach us, all our souls to pour
In high-souled, earnest, heaven-uplifted prayer
To Him who doth alike for all His children care.

G. W.

STANZAS TO TWO EARLY VIOLETS.

TWINS of the spring
    What airs of wood-wild sweets
    Lurk in your fragrant leaves!
    What dreams ye bring
Of early nameless joys that youth first greets,
    Ere time the heart bereaves
    Of all its gladness!

    Oh! vague delight,
    Which hails the vernal day
    Of youthful flowery morn,
    With hopes as bright
As Nature's robe is gorgeously gay,
    Ere the fresh heart is worn
    By withering sadness.

    Oh! vague delight!
    No more in after-day
    Ye ever can return ;
    A mildewed blight

Obscures the brightness of that matin ray,
    And then we just discern
      Our joys were madness.

      Children of Spring !
    Yet still your blossoms bear
    Power of refined delight ;
      Ye bid me sing
Of dreams and days the vulgar cannot share;
    In fortune's proud despite
    I give thee welcoming.

ANON.

A THOUGHT OF THE DAISY

WHEN IN BRAZIL.

I WANDER alone, and often look
For the primrose bank by the rippling brook ;
Which wakened to life by vernal beams,
An emblem of youth and beauty seems,
And I ask where the violet and daisy grow !
But a breeze-borne voice, in whisperings low,
Swept from the north o'er southern seas
Tells me I'm far from the land of these.

GARDNER.

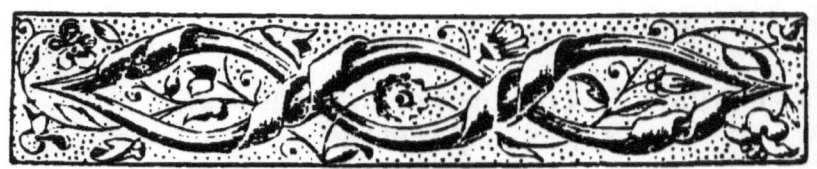

LOVE SHUT OUT OF THE FLOWER-GARDEN.

CLOSE the porch and bar the door !
  Onward may thy footsteps stray :
Never more in idle hour
  Bend thou here thy treacherous way.

Heart's-ease trembles all around,
  As thy wild breath wanders by;
Roses to thy bosom bound—
  Yield their latest, sweetest sigh.

Cruel boy !—abjured and scorned,
  Here thy blushing trophies glow;
Love-lies-bleeding all around—
  Speed thee ! dangerous vagrant ;— go !

Where yon fountain sparkles clear,
  Low beneath its willowy shade,
Nurslings of one parent born,
  Love and idleness have played.

Where yon wild-rose flaunts her flowers,
   (Once its garlands bound my hair,)
Changed for me those sunny hours,
   Thou thy thorn hast planted there.

Frailest woodbine, all untwined,
   Wanders here forlorn and free ;
Emblem of the maiden's mind,
   Who has placed her trust in thee.

How, within my calm retreat,
   Could thy truant footsteps stray ?
Bowed beneath thy breath's control,
   Did my steadiest fence give way.

Passion's-flowers are past and gone ;
   Still around one lovely spot,
All her turquoise gems unchanged,
   Blooms the meek Forget-me-not.

Once, beneath thy fickle power,
   Glowed the hour, or gloomed the day ;
Now my chastened bosom owns
   Wisdom's rule and reason's sway.

Leave me to my new found peace ;
   Leave me to my late repose :
Here at length my troubles cease—
   Here my heart forgets its woes.

Joy of purer influence born,
　Hope of loftier aim I know—
Now thy stormy power I scorn:
　Leave me, child !—thou needs must go.

Art thou fled without a word?
　Closed the porch and barred the door:
Are thy loved companions gone?
　Fair-haired youth had flown before.

Must I from each idol part;
　To each transport bid adieu,
Which around my youthful heart
　Once its blest delusions threw?

Yet sweet Love ! with tears and grief,
　I thy wings receding see;
Sorrow still on parting waits,—
　Hope and joy retire with thee !

RODERIGO COTTA—translated by
MRS. LAWRENCE.

———◆———

SWEET PEAS.

SWEET peas, on tiptoe for a flight
With wings of gentle flush o'er delicate white,
And taper fingers, catching at all things
To bind them round about with tiny rings.

KEATS.

ON A FADED VIOLET.

THE odour from the flower is gone;
  Which, like thy kisses, breathed on me!
The colour from the flower is flown,
  Which glowed of thee, and only thee:

A shrivelled, lifeless, vacant form,
  It lies on my abandoned breast,
And mocks the heart which yet is warm,
  With cold and silent rest.

I weep—my tears revive it not!
  I sigh—it breathes no more on me;
Its mute and uncomplaining lot
  Is such as mine should be.

SHELLEY.

———◆———

CRUSH not the flower while yet it blooms,
  Nor cast in scorn its sweets away,
That breathe around such rich perfumes,
  But with its love will soon decay.
Crush not the tender flower of love,
  Nor rudely tear it from thy heart;
Oh! never may the star above
  By darkening clouds from view depart.

THE FIRST MORNING OF SPRING.

BREAK from your chains, ye lingering streams;
  Rise, blossoms, from your wintry dreams;
  Drear fields, your robes of verdure take;
Birds, from your trance of silence wake;
Glad trees, resume your leafy crown;
Shrubs, o'er the mirror-brooks bend down;
Bland zephyrs, whereso'er ye stray,
The Spring doth call you,—come away.
Thou, too, my soul, with quickened force
Pursue thy brief, thy measured course;
With grateful zeal each power employ;
Catch vigour from Creation's joy;
And deeply, on thy shortening span,
Stamp love to God and love to man.

But Spring, with tardy step appears,
Chill is her eye, and dim with tears;
Still are the founts in fetters bound,—
The flower-germs shrink within the ground.

Where are the warblers of the sky?
I ask,—and angry blasts reply.
It is not thus in heavenly bowers :—
Nor ice-bound rill nor drooping flowers,
Nor silent harp, nor folded wing,
Invade that everlasting Spring
Toward which we look with wishful tear,
While pilgrims in this wintry sphere.

SIGOURNEY.

SONNET.

TO THE CAMELIA JAPONICA.

SAY, what impels me, pure and spotless flower,
   To view thee with a secret sympathy?
   —Is there some living spirit shrined in thee?
That, as thou bloom'st within my humble bower,
Endows thee with some strange mysterious power,
   Waking high thoughts?—As there perchance might
     be
Some angel form of truth and purity,
Whose hallowed presence shared my lonely hour?
   —Yes, lovely flower, 'tis not thy virgin glow,
   Thy petals whiter than descending snow,
Nor all the charms thy velvet folds display,
   'Tis the soft image of some beaming mind,
   By grace adorn'd, by elegance refin'd,
That o'er my heart thus holds its silent sway.

W. ROSCOE.

SPRING IN NEW YORK.

THE country ever has a lagging Spring,
   Waiting for May to call its violets forth,
    And June its roses—showers and sunshine
       bring
Slowly the deepening verdure o'er the earth;
To put their foliage out the woods are slack,
And one by one the singing birds come back.

Within the city's bounds the time of flowers
   Comes earlier.   Let a mild and sunny day,
Such as full often, for a few bright hours,
   Breathes through the sky of March the airs of May,
Shine on our roofs and chase the wintry gloom,
And, lo! our borders glow with sudden bloom.

For the wide side-walks of Broadway are then
   Gorgeous as are a rivulet's bank in June,
That overhung with blossoms, through its glen,
   Slides soft away beneath the sunny noon,

And they who search the untrodden wood for flowers,
Meet in its depths no lovelier ones than ours.

For here are eyes that shame the violet,
   Or the dark drop that on the pansy lies,
And foreheads white as, when in clusters set,
   The anemones by forest fountains rise ;
And the spring-beauty boasts no tenderer stieak
Than the soft red on many a youthful cheek.

And thick about those lovely temples lie
   Locks that the lucky Vignardonne has curled,
Thrice happy man ! whose trade it is to buy,
   And bake, and braid those love-knots of the world,
Who curls of every glossy colour keepest,
And sellest, it is said, the blackest cheapest.

And well thou may'st—for Italy's brown maids
   Send the dark locks with which their brows are
      dressed ;
And Gascon lasses, from their jetty braids,
   Crop half, to buy a riband for the rest :
But the fresh Norman girls their tresses spare,
And the Dutch damsel keeps her flaxen hair.

Then, henceforth, let no maid nor matron grieve,
   To see her locks of an unlovely hue,
Frowsy or thin, for liberal art shall give
   Such piles of curls as nature never knew :
Eve, with her veil of tresses, at the sight
Had blushed outdone, and owned herself a fright.

Soft voices and light laughter wake the street,
   Like notes of woodbirds, and, where'er the eye
Threads the long way, plumes wave, and twinkling
     feet
   Fall light, as hastes the crowd of beauty by;
The ostrich, hurrying o'er the desert space,
Scarce bore those tossing plumes with fleeter pace.

No swimming Juno gait, of languor born,
   Is theirs, but a light step of freest grace,
Light as Camilla's o'er the unbent corn,
   A step that speaks the spirit of the place,
Since Quiet, meek old dame, was driven away
To Sing-Sing and the shores of Tappan bay.

Ye that dash by in chariots ! who will care
   For steeds or footmen now? ye cannot show
Fair face, and dazzling dress, and graceful air,
   And last edition of the shape !   Ah, no,
These sights are for the earth and open sky,
And your loud wheels unheeded rattle by.

                             BRYANT.

THE VIOLET.

WEET lowly plant! once more I bend
    To hail thy presence here,
Like a beloved returning friend,
    From absence doubly dear.

Wert thou for ever in our sight,
    Might we not love thee less?
But now thou bringest new delight,
    Thou still hast power to bless.

Still doth thy April presence bring
    Of April joys a dream,
When life was in its sunny spring—
    A fair unrippled stream.

And still thine exquisite perfume
    Is precious as of old:
And still thy modest tender bloom,
    It joys me to behold.

It joys and cheers, whene'er I see
   Pain on earth's meek ones press,
To think the storm that rends the tree
   Scathes not thy lowliness.

And thus may human weakness find,
   E'en in thy lowly flower,
An image cheering to the mind
   In many a trying hour.

ANON.

SONNET.

BRIGHT rose! that on my father's honoured vest
Hath shed sweet perfume,—breathing o'er his sense
The gales and odours Spring's young suns dispense
O'er opening flowers, in early fragrance drest;—
Bright rose! now sacred are thy fading leaves,
And dear thy wither'd stem; for thou dost tell
Of hours of peace and love remember'd well,—
A father's love, of which time ne'er bereaves.
Oh! be it mine, on this autumnal day,
Like thee to shed delights and sweetly cheer
The lingering hours of the declining year,
And keep cold winter's blast long, long away;
So like thy fragrant flower shall thought of me
Unto his soul sweetness and sunshine be.

J. E. R.

THE KNIGHT AND LADY FAIR.

TOGETHER they sate by a river's side,
    A knight and a lady gay,
And they watched the deep and eddying tide
    Round a flowery islet stray.

And, "Oh for that flower of brilliant hue,"
    Said then the lady fair,
"To grace my neck with the blossoms blue,
    And braid my nut-brown hair!"

The knight has plunged in the whirling wave
    All for his lady's smile:
And he swims the stream with courage brave,
    And he gains yon flowery isle.

And his fingers have cropped the blossoms blue,
    And the prize they backward bear;
To deck his love with the brilliant hue
    And deck her nut-brown hair.

But the way is long and the current strong,
  And alas for that gallant knight !
For the waves prevail and his stout arms fail,
  Though cheered by his lady's sight.

Then the blossoms blue to the bank he threw,
  Ere he sank in the eddying tide!
And "Lady, I'm gone, thine own true knight,—
  Forget me not !" he cried.

This farewell pledge the lady caught ;
  And hence, as legends say,
The flower is a sign to awaken thought
  In friends who are far away.

For the lady fair of her knight so true,
  Still remembered the hapless lot ;
And she cherished the flower of brilliant hue,
And she braided her hair with the blossoms blue,
  And then called it " Forget-me-not !"

                              BISHOP MANT.

DAFFODILS.

 WANDERED lonely as a cloud
That floats on high o'er vales and hills,
When all at once I saw a crowd,
A host of golden daffodils,
Beside the lake, beneath the trees,
Fluttering and dancing in the breeze.

Continuous as the stars that shine
And twinkle in the milky-way,
They stretched in never-ending line
Along the margin of a bay.
Ten thousand saw I at a glance,
Tossing their heads in sprightly dance.

The waves beside them danced; but they
Outdid the sparkling waves in glee:
A poet could not but be gay,
In such a jocund company;
I gazed—and gazed—but little thought
What wealth the show to me had brought:

For oft when on my couch I lie,
In vacant or in pensive mood,
They flash upon that inward eye
Which is the bliss of solitude;
And then my heart with pleasure fills,
And dances with the daffodils.

WORDSWORTH.

———◆———

LOVE'S BED OF STATE.

CUPID nestles in the rose;
　　Well he may! well he may!
Sporting dalliance with repose,
　　Where he slumbers, lapped elate,
　　Breathing odours exquisite;
Round the blushing leaves, all close,
　　Curtaining Love's bed of state!
　　　　　　　　　Well-a-day!

Lulled by song of humming bee!
　　Lullaby! lullaby!
Dreaming plaguish witchery.
　　Alack! the lover hath a heart,
　　Cupid's arrow hath a dart,
And the bee a sting, with his honey,
　　And the rose a thorn, and love a smart!
　　　　　　　　Alack-a-day!

DANIEL.

A WEE FLOWER.

A BONNIE wee flower grew green in the wuds,
Like a twinkling wee star amang the cluds;
And the langer it leevit, the greener it grew,
For 'twas lulled by the winds, and fed by the dew,
Oh! fresh was the air where it reared its head,
Wi' the radiance and odour its young leaves shed.

When the morning sun rose frae his eastern ha',
This bonnie wee flower was the earliest of a'
To open its cups sealed up in the dew,
And spread out its leaves o' the yellow and blue

When the winds were still and the sun rode high,
And the clear mountain stream ran whimpling by,
When the wee birds sang, and the wilderness bee
Was floating awa', like a clud o'er the sea;
This bonnie wee flower was blooming unseen—
The sweet child of summer—in its rokelay green.

And when the night clud grew dark on the plain,
When the stars were out, and the moon in the wane,
When the bird and the bee had gane to rest,
And the dews of the night the green earth press'd,
This bonnie wee flower lay smiling asleep,
Like a beautiful pearl in the dark green deep.

And when autumn came, and the summer had pass'd,
And the wan leaves were strewn on the twirling blast,
This bonnie wee flower grew naked and bare,
And its wee leaves shrank in the frozen air;
Wild darnel and nettle sprang rank from the ground,
But the rose and the wild lilies were drooping around,
And this bonnie blue flower hung doon its wee head,
And the bright morning sun flung its beams on its bed;
And the pale stars looked forth—but the wee flower was
    dead.

ANDERSON.

THE BROKEN FLOWER.

OH! wear it on thy heart, my love!
   Still, still a little while!
Sweetness is lingering in its leaves,
   Though faded be their smile.
Yet for the sake of what hath been,
   Oh! cast it not away!
'Twas born to grace a summer scene,
   A long bright golden day,
          My love!
   A long bright golden day!

A little while around thee, love!
   Its fragrance yet shall cling,
Telling that on thy heart hath lain,
   A fair though faded thing.
But not even that warm heart hath power
   To win it back from fate.—
Oh! I am like that broken flower,
   Cherished too late, too late,
          My love!
   Cherished, alas! too late!

HEMANS.

A THOUGHT OF THE ROSE.

HOW much of memory dwells amidst thy bloom,
　　Rose! ever wearing beauty for thy dower!
　The Bridal day—the Festival—the Tomb—
Thou hast thy part in each,—thou stateliest flower!

Therefore with thy soft breath come floating by
　A thousand images of Love and Grief,
Dreams, fill'd with tokens of mortality,
　Deep thoughts of all things beautiful and brief,

Not such thy spells o'er those that hail'd thee first
　In the clear light of Eden's golden day;
There thy rich leaves to crimson glory burst,
　Link'd with no dim remembrance of decay.

Rose! for the banquet gather'd, and the bier;
　Rose! coloured now by human hope or pain,
Surely, where death is not—nor change, nor fear,
　Yet may we meet thee, Joy's own Flower, again!

　　　　　　　　　　　　　　　　MRS. HEMANS.

HEART'S-EASE.

IN gardens oft a beauteous flower there grows,
  By vulgar eyes unnoticed and unseen;
In sweet security it humbly blows,
  And rears its purple head to deck the green.

This flower, as Nature's poet sweetly sings,
  Was once milk-white, and Heart's-ease was its name,
Till wanton Cupid poised his roseate wings,
  A vestal's sacred bosom to inflame.

With treacherous aim the god his arrow drew,
  Which she with icy coldness did repel;
Rebounding thence with feathery speed it flew,
  Till on this lonely flower, at last, it fell.

Heart's-ease no more the wandering shepherd found;
  No more the nymphs its snowy form possess;
Its white now changed to purple by Love's wound,
  Heart's-ease no more,—tis Love-in-idleness.

MRS. SHERIDAN.

HEART'S-EASE.

 USED to love thee, simple flower,
  To love thee dearly when a boy;
For thou didst seem in childhood's hour,
  The smiling type of childhood's joy.

But now thou only work'st my grief,
  By waking thoughts of pleasures fled.
Give me, give me the withered leaf,
  That falls on Autumn's bosom dead.

For that ne'er tells of what has been,
  But warns me what I soon shall be;
It looks not back on pleasure's scene,
  But points unto futurity.

I love thee not, thou simple flower,
  For thou art gay, and I am lone;
Thy beauty died with childhood's hour—
  The heart's-ease from my path is gone.

                                        ANON.

THE BEE AND THE LADY-FLOWER.

A S Julia once a slumbering lay,
   It chanced a bee did fly that way,
   After a dew, or dew-like shower,
To tipple freely in a flower.
For some rich flower he took the lip
Of Julia, and began to sip;
But when he felt he sucked from thence
Honey, and in the quintessence,
He drank so much he scarce could stir,
So Julia took the pilferer,
And thus surprised, as filchers use,
He thus began to make excuse:
Sweet Lady-flower, I never brought
Hither the least one thieving thought;
But taking these rare lips of yours
For some fresh, fragrant, luscious flowers,
I thought I might there take a taste,
Where so much syrup ran at waste,

Besides, know this, I never sting
The flower that gives me nourishing;
But with a kiss, or thanks, do pay
For honey that I bear away.
This said, he laid his little scrip
Of honey 'fore her ladyship :
And told her, as some tears did fall,
That that he took, and that was all.
At which she smiled, and bad him go
And take his bag ; but this much know,
When next he came a-pilfering so,
He should from her full lips derive
Honey enough to fill his hive.

HERRICK.

SONG OF THE CAPTIVE.

FROM THE GERMAN OF GOETHE.

CAPTIVE.

A FLOWER that's wondrous fair, I know,
　My bosom holds it dear;
To seek that flower I long to go,
　But am imprisoned here.
'Tis no light grief oppresses me;
For, in the days my steps were free,
　I had it always near.
Far round the tower I send mine eye,
　The tower so steep and tall!
But nowhere can the flower descry
　From this high castle wall;
And him who'll bring me my desire,
Or be he knight or be he squire,
　My dearest friend I'll call.

ROSE.

My blossoms near thee I disclose,
　And hear thy wretched plight;

Thou meanest me, no doubt,—the rose,
Thou noble, hapless knight.
A lofty mind in thee is seen,
And in thy bosom reigns the queen
Of flowers, as is her right.

CAPTIVE.

Thy crimson bud I duly prize,
In outer robe of green;
For this thou'rt dear in maiden's eyes,
As gold and jewels' sheen.
Thy wreath adorns the fairest brow,
And yet the flower—it is not thou,
Whom my still wishes mean.

LILY.

The little rose has cause of pride,
And upwards aye will soar;
Yet am I held by many a bride
The rose's wreath before.
And beats thy bosom faithfully,
And art thou true, and pure as I,
Thou'lt prize the lily more.

CAPTIVE.

I call myself both chaste and pure,
And free from passions low;
And yet these walls my limbs immure
In loneliness and woe.

Though thou dost seem in white arrayed,
Like many a pure and beauteous maid,
   One dearer thing I know.

PINK.

And dearer I, the pink, must be,
   And me thou sure dost choose,
Or else the gardener ne'er for me
   Such watchful care would use;
A crowd of leaves enriching bloom !
And mine through life the sweet perfume,
   And all the thousand hues.

CAPTIVE.

The pink, can no one justly slight,
   The gardener's favourite flower ;
He sets it now beneath the light,
   Now shields it from its power ;
Yet, 'tis not pomp, who o'er the rest
In splendour shines, can make me blest ;
   It is a still small flower.

VIOLET.

I stand concealed, and bending low,
   And do not love to speak ;
Yet will I, as 'tis fitting now,
   My wonted silence break.
For if 'tis I, thou gallant man,
Thy heart desires, thine, if I can,
   My perfumes all I'll make.

The Forget-me-Not.

CAPTIVE.

The violet I esteem indeed,
   So modest and so kind;
Its fragrance sweet yet more I need,
   To soothe mine anguished mind.
To you the truth will I confess;
Here, 'mid this rocky dreariness,
   My love I ne'er shall find.

The truest wife by yonder brook
   Will roam the mournful day,
And hither cast the anxious look,
   Long as immured I stay.
Whene'er she breaks a small blue flower,
And says " Forget me not!" the power
   I feel, though far away.

Yes, e'en though far, I feel its might,
   For true love joins us twain,
And therefore 'mid the dungeon's night
   I still in life remain.
And sinks my heart at my hard lot,
I but exclaim " Forget-me-not!"
   And straight new life regain.

                   ANON.

THE ALMOND TREE.

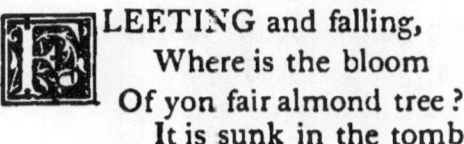LEETING and falling,
  Where is the bloom
Of yon fair almond tree?
  It is sunk in the tomb.

Its tomb, wheresoever
  The wind may have borne
The leaves and the blossoms,
  Its roughness has torn.

Some there are floating
  On yon fountain's breast;
Some line the moss
  Of the nightingale's nest.

Some are just strewn
  O'er the green grass below,
And there they lie stainless
  As winter's first snow.

The Forget-me-Not.

Yesterday on the boughs
  They hung scented and fair :
To-day they are scattered
  The breeze best knows where.

To-morrow, those leaves
  Will be scentless and dead,
For the kind to lament
  And the careless to tread.

And is it not thus
  With each hope of the heart?
With all its best feelings,
  Thus will they depart.

They'll go forth to the world
  On the wings of the air,
Rejoicing and hoping,
  But what will be there ?

False lights to deceive,
  False friends to delude,
Till the heart, in its sorrow,
  Left only to brood—

Over feelings, crushed, chilled,
  Sweet hopes ever flown ;
Like that tree, when its green leaves
  And blossoms are gone.
                              MISS LANDON.

LINES

ON RECEIVING A BRANCH OF MEZEREON.

ODOURS of spring, my sense ye charm,
    With fragrance premature,
And 'mid these days of dark alarm,
    Almost to hope allure.
Methinks with purpose soft ye come,
    To tell of brighter hours,
Of May's blue skies, abundant bloom,
    Her sunny gales and showers.

Alas ! for me shall May in vain
    The powers of life restore ;
These eyes that weep and watch in pain,
    Shall see her charms no more.
No, no, this anguish cannot last ;
    Beloved friends, adieu ;
The bitterness of death were past,
    Could I resign but you.

Oh! ye who soothe the pangs of death
   With love's own patient care,
Still, still retain this fleeting breath,
   Still pour the fervent prayer.
And ye whose smiles must greet my eye
   No more, nor voice my ear,
Who breathe for me the tender sigh,
   And shed the pitying tear;

Whose kindness, though far, far removed,
   My grateful thoughts perceive;
Pride of my life—esteemed, beloved,
   My last sad claim receive!
Oh, do not quite your friend forget—
   Forget alone her faults;
And speak of her with fond regret,
   Who asks your lingering thoughts.

               Mrs. Tighe.

SONG.

LASSIE, let us stray together,
    Far from town or tower;
O'er the mountain, where the heather
    Spreads its purple flower:—
Princely halls were made for pride,
    Towns for low deceit, dear Lassie!—
'Tis but near the brae's green side,
    Thou and I should meet, dear Lassie!

Where the mountain-daisy's blowing
    On the turf we tread,
Where the rippling burn is flowing
    O'er its pebbly bed,
There—while ev'ry opening flower
    As thy smile is sweet, dear Lassie!
Shelter'd in some leafy bower,
    Thou and I should meet, dear Lassie!

SUMMER FLOWERS.

WELCOME, O pure and lowly forms, again
Unto the shadowy stillness of my room !
For not alone ye bring a joyous train
Of summer thoughts attendant on your bloom ;
Visions of freshness, of rich bowery gloom,
Of the low murmurs filling mossy dells,
Of stars that look down on your folded bells;
Through dewy leaves, of many a wild perfume,
Greeting the wanderer of hill and grove
Like sudden music; more than this ye bring—
Far more; ye whisper of the fost'ring love,
Which has thus clothed you, and whose dove-like wing
Broods o'er the sufferer, drawing fevered breath,
Whether the couch be that of life or death.

MRS. HEMANS.

THE BLIND FLOWER-GIRL'S SONG.

UY my flowers, O buy, I pray,
    The blind girl comes from far;
If the earth be as fair as I hear them say,
    These flowers her children are!
Do they her beauty keep?
    They are fresh from her lap, I know,
For I caught them fast asleep
    In her arms, an hour ago,
With the air which is her breath,
Her soft and delicate breath,
    Over them murmuring low.
On their lips her sweet kiss lingers yet,
And their cheeks with her tender tears are wet;
For she weeps, that gentle mother weeps,
As morn and night her watch she keeps,
With a yearning heart and a passionate care;—
To see the young things grow so fair;
    She weeps—for love she weeps,
    And the dews are the tears she weeps
        From the well of a mother's love.

Ye have a world of light
  Where love in the loved rejoices,
But the blind girl's home is the house of night,
  And its beings are empty voices.
    As one in the realm below
  I stand by the streams of woe,
  I hear the vain shadows glide,
  I feel their soft breath at my side,
And I thirst their loved forms to see,
  And I stretch my fond arms around,
  And I catch but a shapeless sound.
    For the living are ghosts to me.
  Come buy! come buy!
Hark how the sweet things sigh,
For they have a voice like ours,—
" The breath of the blind girl closes
" The leaves of the saddening roses:
" We are, we are sons of light,
" We shrink from this child of night:
" From the grasp of the blind girl free us,
" We yearn for the eyes that see us,
" We are for the night too gay,
" In your eyes we behold the day."
—O buy,—O buy the flowers !

BULWER.

REMEMBRANCE.

REMEMBRANCE! oh the crowd of thoughts
that word doth comprehend!—
Thoughts burning in the lover's heart, or in the
breast of friend;
Thoughts now o'ercharged with heaviness, now big with
life and light,
Upborne on wings of ripened hopes, or laden with their
blight;
Now fresh in healthful glow,
Now withering as they grow;—
Oh! who shall paint REMEMBRANCE in its blended bliss
and woe?

REMEMBRANCE! oh! 'tis blessed, when the retrospective
glance
Lends but a brighter beam to days and years as they ad-
vance,
When present joys win richer zest from former doubts
and fears,
And we reap a smiling harvest from a seed-time past of
tears;

Like lovers' healing kiss,
In semblance such as this,
Thou art in sooth, REMEMBRANCE, but another name for
bliss.

REMEMBRANCE! ah, 'tis wretched, when its meditations
bring
Fresh and alive to view no forms but such as wound and
sting;
Bright prospects faded; kindness wronged; warm confi-
dence betrayed;
Affection scorned; and friendship—but the shadow of a
shade;
Alas! in such a dress,
Fit partner of distress,
Alas! what can REMEMBRANCE be, but added wretched-
ness?

REMEMBRANCE! where's the mortal who unshrinking
has withstood
Temptation of the evil one, and held his course of good;
Has spurned the crooked bye-path, put aside the gilded
sin,
Unswayed by other voices than the still small voice
within?—
Arrayed in robes of light,
Him doth REMEMBRANCE bright
Visit in cheering thoughts by day and placid dreams by
night.

REMEMBRANCE! Ask of him who yields up principle for
    place,
And barters simple honour for magnificent disgrace;
Ask her whose treachery dooms a trusting heart to pine
    to death;
Ask him who love and service true requites—with empty
    breath;
  Can power, rank, wealth, appease
  The conscious mind's disease?
Ask what, in still reflection's hour, REMEMBRANCE says
    to these.

REMEMBRANCE! What is it to him, the slave of power's
    pretext,
The favourite of this hour's caprice, the victim of the
    next;
A banished man—compelled in bitter listlessness to roam
Afar from home and friends and love, and all that *makes*
    it home;
  Oh say, to such as he
  What can REMEMBRANCE be,
But aggravated sentence of an inward misery?

REMEMBRANCE! Aye to him who borne in manhood's
    healthful pride
O'er Danube's wave, or Tiber's stream, or Ganges'
    swollen tide,

From palace or from fort, from classic arch or trophied
    dome,
Looks through a lengthened vista to the dear-loved scenes
    of home,
    Nor feels the wish is vain
    To mix in them again ;—
To him REMEMBRANCE brings a pleasure unalloyed
    by pain.

REMEMBRANCE ! Thou who readest, hast thou had what's
    called a friend ?
A smiling one, a summer one? Hast seen the summer's
    end ?
Hast marked with Fortune's changing front this friend's
    as changing face,
This would-be-thought so faithful one, while all was false
    and base ;
    His hollow forced respect,
    His real mean neglect?
One needs not ask how *thou* dost feel REMEMBRANCE, I
    suspect.

REMEMBRANCE !—Sinking worth upraised, unfriended
    merit reared,
The wretched soothed, the orphan fed, the heart of widow
    cheered ;
The friend not coldly viewed because assisted from thy
    store,
But all life's gentle courtesies thence only shown the
    more ;—

Whom thoughts like these attend,
  To life's remotest end
REMEMBRANCE bears them company, a comforter and
  friend.

REMEMBRANCE! Fathom he who can wnat thoughts *his*
  bosom swell
Who mourns the altered bearing of the one he loved so
  well ;
The beaming eye, the witching smile, the voice so rich,
  so kind,
Looks, words, hopes, promises, all gone, all scattered to
  the wind ;—
  His cup is filled to th' brim ;
  And on its murky rim
REMEMBRANCE sits—oh ask not *what* REMEMBRANCE is
  to him.

REMEMBRANCE! oh 'tis made of paintul thoughts and
  blissful too,
As autumn skies, now low'ring dark, now bright with
  heavenly blue ;
But this our consolation, that in stormy sky or fair,
In sunshine or in darkness, still a PROVIDENCE is there ;
  That still, come cloud, come ray,
  Come wind, "come what come may,"
God and an honest heart will bring us through the
  roughest day.

                                        T. G. A.

HOME.

IS this no dream, and do I see
    My own paternal cot once more?
How could I think that heaven for me
    Reserved no happy lot in store!
Come, then, prepare the festal lay—
    And bid the sparkling wine cup foam;
Let mirth and music grace the day
    Which brings the weary wanderer home.

Oh! I have been an exile long,
    Have crossed Arabia's sultry sands,
Have pass'd through Greece, renown'd in song,
    And seen Columbia's fertile lands,
Have mark'd Italian sunsets glow
    On many a lofty tower and dome;
Yet is there not one splendid show
    Can give delight like welcome home.

I hear the humming of the bees;
　The murmuring warblers tell their tale,
Among the branches of the trees
　That blossom round my own green vale.
Here I will draw my latest breath;
　Beyond this spot no more I'll roam;
And, oh! my spirit, after death,
　Shall wan 'er round my native home.

RICHARD HILL.

SONG OF THE FORGET-ME-NOT.

How many bright flowers now around me are glancing,
Each seeking its praise, or its beauty enhancing!
The rose-buds are hanging like gems in the air,
And the lily-bell waves in her fragrance there.
　Alas! I can claim neither fortune nor power,
　Neither beauty nor fragrance are cast in my lot;
　But contented I cling to my lowly bower,
　And smile while I whisper—'*Forget-me-not!*'

SWISS HOME-SICKNESS.

TRANSLATED FROM THE LAST OF THE MELODIES SUNG BY
THE TYROLESE FAMILY.

"Herz, mein Herz, warum so traurig," &c.

HEREFORE so sad and faint, my heart?—
    The stranger's land is fair;
Yet weary, weary still thou art—
    What find'st thou wanting there?

What wanting?—all, oh! all I love!
    Am I not lonely here?
Through a fair land in sooth I rove,
    Yet what like home is dear?

My home! oh! thither would I fly,
    Where the free air is sweet,
My father's voice, my mother's eye,
    My own wild hills to greet.

My hills, with all their soaring steeps,
    With all their glaciers bright,
Where in his joy the chamois leaps,
    Mocking the hunter's might.

Oh! but to hear the herd-bell sound,
  When shepherds lead the way
Up the high Alps, and children bound,
  And not a lamb will stray!

Oh! but to climb the uplands free,
  And, where the pure streams foam,
By the blue shining lake, to see,
  Once more, my hamlet-home!

Here, no familiar look I trace;
  I touch no friendly hand;
No child laughs kindly in my face—
  As in my own bright land!

Mrs. Hemans.

AS IT FELL UPON A DAY.

A S it fell upon a day,
In the merry month of May,
Sitting in a pleasant shade
Which a grove of myrtles made,
Beasts did leap, and birds did sing,
Trees did grow, and plants did spring:
Everything did banish moan,
Save the nightingale alone:
She, poor bird, as all forlorn,
Lean'd her breast against a thorn,
And there sung the dolefull'st ditty,
That to hear it was great pity:
Fie, fie, fie, now would she cry,
Teru, teru, by and by:
That to hear her so complain,
Scarce I could from tears refrain;
For her griefs so lively shown,
Made me think upon mine own.
Ah! (thought I) thou mourn'st in vain;
None take pity on thy pain:

Senseless trees, they cannot hear thee;
Ruthless bears, they will not cheer thee,
King Pandion, he is dead;
All thy friends are lapp'd in lead:
All thy fellow birds do sing,
Careless of thy sorrowing.
Even so, poor bird, like thee,
None alive will pity me.
Whilst as fickle fortune smiled,
Thou and I were both beguiled.
Everyone that flatters thee,
Is no friend in misery.
Words are easy like the wind;
Faithful friends are hard to find.
Every man will be thy friend,
Whilst thou hast wherewith to spend:
But if store of crowns be scant,
No man will supply thy want.
If that one be prodigal,
Bountiful they will him call:
And with such-like flattering,
" *Pity but he were a king.*"

*   *   *   *   *

Buf if fortune once do frown,
Then farewell his great renown:
They that fawn'd on him before,
Use his company no more.
He that is thy friend indeed,
He will help thee in thy need,

If thou sorrow, he will weep;
If thou wake, he cannot sleep:
Thus of every grief in heart
He with thee doth bear a part.
These are certain signs to know
Faithful friend from flattering foe.

SHAKSPEARE.

———◆———

PHILOCTETES.

WHEN Philoctetes, in the Lemnian isle,
  Like a form sculptured on a monument,
  Lay couched, on him or his dread bow unbent
Some wild bird oft might settle, and beguile
The rigid features of a transient smile,
  Disperse the tear, or to the sigh give vent,
  Slackening the pains of ruthless banishment
From his loved home, and from heroic toil.
  And trust that spiritual creatures round us move,
Griefs to allay which reason cannot heal;
  Yea, veriest reptiles have sufficed to prove
To fettered wretchedness, that no Bastile
  Is deep enough to exclude the light of love,
Though man for brother man has ceased to feel.

WORDSWORTH.

THE LOTUS.

HOW sweet it were, hearing the downward stream
   With half-shut eyes ever to seem
   Falling asleep in a half dream !
To dream and dream, like yonder amber light,
Which will not leave the myrrh bush on the height;
To hear each other's whispered speech;
   Eating the Lotus, day by day,
To watch the crisping ripples on the beach,
   And tender curving lines of creamy spray;
To lend our hearts and spirits wholly
To the influence of mild-minded melancholy;
To muse and brood and live again in memory,
With those old faces of our infancy
Heaped over with a mound of grass,
Two handfuls of white dust, shut in an urn of brass.
   The Lotus blooms below the flowery peak ;
   The Lotus blows by every winding creek ;
All day the wind breathes low, with mellower tone ;
Through every hollow cave and alley lone,

Round and round the spicy downs the yellow Lotus dust
  is blown.

We have had enough of action and of motion, we

Rolled to starboard, rolled to larboard, when the surge was
  seething free,

Where the wallowing monster spouted his foam fountains
  in the sea.

Let us swear an oath, and keep it with an equal mind,

In the hollow Lotus land to live and lie reclined

On the hills like gods together, careless of mankind ;

For they lie beside their nectar, and the bolts are hurled

Far below them in the valleys, and the clouds are lightly
  curled

Round their golden houses, girdled with the gleaming
  world.

Surely, surely slumber is more sweet than toil; the
  shore

Than labour in the deep, mid ocean, wind and wave and
  oar ;

O, rest ye, brother mariners ; we will not wander more.

TENNYSON.

THE GRECIAN MAIDENS REMEMBER
SAPPHO.

WHEN evening came, around the well
    They sate, beneath the rising moon,
And some, with voice of awe could tell
Of midnight's fays and nymphs who dwell
    In holy fountains; some would tune
Their lutes to sounds of softest close,
To tell of Sappho's love and woes.

Among these maidens there was one
    Who to Leucadia late had been,—
Had stood beneath the evening sun
    On its white, towering cliffs, and seen
The very spot where Sappho sung
Her swan-like music, ere she sprung
(Still holding in that fearful leap
By her loved lyre) into the deep;
And dying quenched the fatal fire,
At once, of both her heart and lyre.

Mutely they listened all; and well
Did the young travelled maiden tell
Of the dread height to which that steep
Beetles above the eddying deep;
Of the lone sea birds, wheeling round
The dizzy edge with mournful sound;
And of the scented lilies, (some
   Of whose white flowers, the damsel said
Herself had gathered, and brought home
   In memory of the minstrel maid,)
Still blooming on that fearful place.

MOORE.

THE SHEPHERD OF KING ADMETUS.

MEN called him but a shiftless youth,
   In whom no good they saw,
And yet unwittingly, in truth,
   They made his careless words their law.
And day by day more holy grew
   Each spot where he had trod,
Till after-poets only knew
   Their first-born brother was a god.

LOWELL.

SAPPHO.

FROM A GEM.

LOOK on this brow! The laurel wreath
　　Beamed on it like a wreath of fire;
For passion gave the living breath
　　That shook the chords of Sappho's lyre.

Look on this brow! The lowest slave,
　　The veriest wretch of want and care,
Might shudder at the lot that gave
　　Her genius, glory, and despair.

For from these lips were uttered sighs
　　That, more than fever, scorched the frame;
And tears were rained from these bright eyes,
　　That from the heart like life-blood came.

She loved,—she felt the lightning gleam
　　That keenest strikes the loftiest mind,—
Life quenched in one ecstatic dream,
　　The world a waste, before, behind.

And she had hope—the treacherous hope,
  The last, deep poison of the bowl,
That makes us drain it, drop by drop,
  Nor lose one misery of soul.

Then all gave way—mind, passion, pride;
  She cast one weeping glance above,
Then buried in her bed, the tide,
  The whole concentred strife of love.

CROLY.

CUPID AND PSYCHE.

THEY wove bright fables in the days of old,
    When reason borrowed fancy's painted wings ;
When truth's clear river flowed o'er sands of gold,
And told in song its high and mystic things !
And such the sweet and solemn tale of her,
    The pilgrim heart, to whom a dream was given
That led her through the world—Love's worshipper,—
    To seek on earth for him whose home was heaven !

In the full city,—by the haunted fount,—
    Through the dim grotto's tracery of spars,—
'Mid the pine temples, on the moon-lit mount,
    Where silence sits to listen to the stars ;
In the deep glade where dwells the brooding dove,
    The painted valley, and the scented air,
She heard far echoes of the voice of Love,
    And found his footsteps' traces everywhere.

But never more they met ! since doubts and fears,
  Those phantom shapes that haunt and blight the
    earth,
Had come 'twixt her, a child of sin and tears,
  And that bright spirit of immortal birth ;
Until her pining soul and weeping eyes
Had learned to seek him only in the skies ;
Till wings unto the weary heart were given,
And she became Love's angel bride in heaven !

T. K. HARVEY.

CUPID CARRYING PROVISIONS.

FROM A GEM.

THERE was once a gentle time
Whenne the worlde was in its prime,
And everye day was holydaye,
And everye monthe was lovelie Maye;
Cupid thenne hadde but to goe
Withe his purple winges and bowe,
And in blossomede vale and grove
Everie shepherde knelt to love.

Then a rosie, dimpiede cheeke,
And a blue eye, fonde and meeke,
And a ringlette-wreathenne browe,
Like hyacinthes on a bedde of snowe,
And a lowe voice silverre-sweete,
From a lippe without deceite,
Onlie those the heartes coulde move
Of the simple swaines to love.

But thatte time is gone and paste;
Canne the summerre alwaies laste?

And the swaines are wiser growne,
And the harte is turnede to stone,
And the maidenne's rose maye witherre ;
Cupide's fledde, no manne knowes whitherre.

But another Cupide's come,
With a browe of care and gloome,
Fixed upon the earthlie molde,
Thinkinge of the sullene golde ;
In his hande the bowe no more,
At his backe the householde store
That the bridalle golde muste buye,—
Uselesse now the smile and sighe.
But he weares the pinion stille,
Flyinge at the sighte of ille.
Oh for the olde true-love time
Whenne the worlde was in its prime !

CROLY.

THE ORIGIN OF FABLE.

WHAT has made the sage or poet write
But the fair paradise of Nature's light ?
In the calm grandeur of a sober line,
We see the waving of the mountain pine;
And when a tale is beautifully staid,
We feel the safety of a hawthorn glade.
When it is moving on luxurious wings,
The soul is lost in pleasant smotherings;
Fair dewy roses brush against our faces,
And flowering laurels spring from diamond vases.
O'erhead we see the jasmine and sweetbrier,
And bloomy grapes, laughing from green attire;
While at our feet the voice of crystal bubbles
Charms us at once away from all our troubles;
So that we feel uplifted from the world,
Walking upon the white clouds, wreathed and curled.
So felt he who first told how Psyche went
On the smooth wind to realms of wonderment;
What Psyche felt, and Love, when their full lips
First touched ; what amorous and fondling nips
They gave each other's cheeks; with all their sighs,
And how they kissed each other's tremulous eyes;

The silver lamp,—the ravishment,—the wonder,
The darkness,—loneliness,—the fearful thunder ;
Their woes gone by, and both to heaven upflown,
To bow for gratitude before Jove's throne.

So did he feel who pulled the boughs aside,
That we might look into a forest wide,
Telling us how fair trembling Syrinx fled
Arcadian Pan, with such a fearful dread.
Poor nymph—poor Pan—how he did weep to find
Nought but a lovely sighing of the wind
Along the reedy stream ; a half heard strain,
Full of sweet desolation, balmy pain.

What first inspired a bard of old to sing
Narcissus pining o'er th' untainted spring?
In some delicious ramble, he had found
A little space, with boughs all woven round,
And in the midst of all a clearer pool
Than e'er reflected, in its pleasant cool,
The blue sky, here and there serenely peeping
Through tendril wreaths fantastically creeping.
And on the bank a lonely flower he spied,
A meek and forlorn flower, with nought of pride,
Drooping its beauty o'er the watery clearness,
To woo its own sad image into nearness.
Deaf to light Zephyrus, it would not move,
But still would seem to droop, to pine, to love ;
So while the poet stood in this sweet spot,
Some fainter gleamings o'er his fancy shot ;

Nor was it long ere he had told the tale
Of young Narcissus, and sad Echo's bale.

Where had he been from whose warm head outflew
That sweetest of all songs, that ever-new,
That aye-refreshing, pure deliciousness,
Coming ever to bless
The wanderer by moonlight, to him bringing
Shapes from the invisible world, unearthly singing
From out the middle air, from flowery nests,
And from the pillowy silkiness that rests
Full in the speculation of the stars?
Ah! surely he had burst our mortal bars;
Into some wondrous region he had gone
To search for thee, divine Endymion!

He was a poet, sure a lover too,
Who stood on Latmos' top, what time there blew
Soft breezes from the myrtle vale below;
And brought, in faintness solemn, sweet, and slow,
A hymn from Dian's temple: while upswelling
The incense went to her own starry dwelling.
But though her face was clear as infant's eyes,
Though she stood smiling o'er the sacrifice,
The poet wept at her so piteous fate,
Wept that such beauty should be desolate;
So, in fine wrath, some golden sounds he won,
And gave meek Cynthia her Endymion.

                                   KEATS.

PILGRIMAGE.

VAIN folly of another age,
　　This wandering over earth
To find the peace, by some dark sin
　　Banished our household hearth.

＊　　＊　　＊　　＊　　＊

Return, with prayer and tear return,
　　To those who weep at home;
To dry their tears will more avail,
　　Than o'er a world to roam.

There's hope for one who leaves with shame
　　The guilt that lured before;
Remember, He who said " repent,"
　　Said also " sin no more."

Return! and in thy daily round
　　Of duty and of love,
Thou best wilt find that patient faith
　　Which lifts the soul above.

Around thee draw thine own home ties,
  And with a chastened mind
In meek well-doing seek that peace,
  No wandering will find.

In charity and penitence
  Thy sin will be forgiven;—
Pilgrim! the heart is the true shrine
  Whence prayers ascend to heaven.

MISS LANDON.

A TRUTH.

'Tis the great Spirit, wide diffused
  Through everything we see,
That with our spirits communeth
Of things mysterious—life and death,
  Time and eternity.

ANONYMOUS.

THOUGHTS ON FLOWERS.

NATURE'S eternal jewels!   In old times,
With such as these the peasant girls of Greece
Fill'd high their laps, where the Eurotas strays;
And in far ages, yet unborn and void,
Millions of village maidens will entwine
These starry glories in their dewy hair.
Man dies—but the immortal thoughts of man,
The common feelings of humanity,
Live on the same to-day as yesterday.

A memory of the past—a flower I love—
Not for itself—but that its name is linked
With names I love; and that 'twas once to me
An omen of success, when smilingly
Young friendship said that 'twould be ever so,—
Alas! how vainly!

There is religion in a flower;
Its still small voice is as the voice of conscience:

Mountains and oceans, planets, suns, and systems,
Bear not the impress of Almighty power
In characters more legible than those
Which He hath written on the tiniest flower
Whose light bell bends beneath the dewdrop's weight.

The heart's affections—are they not like flowers?
In life's first spring they blossom ; summer comes,
And 'neath the scorching blaze they droop apace ;
Autumn revives them not : in languid groups
They linger still, perchance, by grove or stream,
But Winter frowns, and gives them to the winds ;
They are all wither'd !

Perchance 'tis very childishness that weaves
Fancies with flowers, and borrows from their hue
A colour for our thoughts ; but if it be,
It is a weakness that will win a smile,
Not tempt a frown, from sage philosophy ;
Or if he frown, in sooth, he's not the sage
Men take him for.   I would not give the love
My heart can feel for this frail harmless thing
Of green and gold, to be enshrined in all
The dusty grandeur of his worm-eat lore.

The Casket.

LIGHT IN DARKNESS.

NIGHT, stern, eternal, and alone,
  Girded with solemn silence round,
Majestic on his starless throne
  Sat brooding o'er the vast profound;
And there unbroken darkness lay,
  Deeper than that which veils the tomb,
While circling ages wheel'd away
  Unnoted 'mid the voiceless gloom.

Then moved upon the waveless deep
  The quickening Spirit of the Lord,
And broken was its pulseless sleep
  Before the Everlasting word—
" Let there be light !" and listening earth,
  With tree, and plant, and flowery sod,
" In the beginning " sprang to birth,
  Obedient to the voice of God.

In glory bathed, the radiant day
  Wore, like a king, his crown of light;
And girdled by the " Milky Way "
  How queenly looked the star-gemmed night !

Bursting from choirs celestial, rang
   Triumphantly the notes of song.

    *   *   *   *   *

Creator! let Thy Spirit shine
   The darkness of our souls within,
And lead us by Thy grace divine
   From the forbidden paths of sin.
And may that voice which bade the earth
   From chaos and the realms of Night—
From doubt and darkness call us forth
   To God's own liberty and light.

Thus made partakers of Thy love,
   The baptism of the Spirit—ours,
Our grateful hearts shall rise above,
   Renewed in purposes and powers.
And songs of joy again shall ring
   Triumphant through the arch of heaven—
The glorious songs which angels sing
   Exulting over souls forgiven.

                    W. H. BURLEIGH.

SELF-KNOWLEDGE.

FOR while the face of outward things we find
   Pleasing and fair, agreeable and sweet,
   These things transport and carry out the mind
That with herself herself can never meet.

    *   *   *   *   *

If ought can teach us ought, affliction's looks,
   Making us look into ourselves more near,
Teach us to know ourselves beyond all books,
   And all the learned schools that ever were.

This mistress lately pluck'd me by the ear,
   And many a golden lesson hath me taught,
Hath made my senses quick, and reason clear,
   Reform'd my will and rectified my thought.

So do the winds and thunder cleanse the air;
   So working lees settle and purge the wine;
So lopp'd and prunéd trees do flourish fair;
   So doth the fire the drossy gold refine.

I know my soul hath power to know all things,
   Yet is she blind and ignorant in all;
I know I'm one of nature's little kings,
   Yet to the least and vilest things am thrall.

                  SIR JOHN DAVIES.

FLOREAL.

BLOSSOMS vernal white,
    Leaves autumnal yellow,
Make the landscape's youth all bright,
    And its age all mellow.

Welcome then each bud!
    Welcome wood and dingle!
Where in nature's ample flood,
    Leaves and blossoms mingle!

Heaven, so Fable tells,
    Hath celestial flowers,
Meads divine of asphodels,
    And amaranthine bowers.

Yet though earth's like reeds
    God hath doom'd to perish,
Beauty lives in world born weeds,
    Beauty gods might cherish.

Welcome then each spray,
  Welcome every bramble;
Welcome budding woods of May,
  Tempting feet to ramble.

KENT.

—THE wise, who soar but never roam,
True to the kindred points of heaven and home.

WORDSWORTH.

JEANIE MORRISON.

I'VE wander'd east, I've wander'd west,
   Through mony a weary way !
But never, never can forget
   The luv o' life's young day.
The fire that's blawn on Beltane e'en
   May weel be black gin Yule ;
But blacker fa' awaits the heart
   Where first fond luve grows cule.

O dear, dear Jeanie Morrison,
   The thochts o' bygane years
Still fling their shadows ower my path,
   And blind my een wi' tears !
They blind my een wi' saut, saut tears,
   And sair and sick I pine,
As memory idly summons up
   The blythe blinks o' langsyne.

'Twas then we luvit ilk ither weel,
   'Twas then we twa did part :
Sweet time—sad time ! twa bairns at schule,
   'Twa bairns and but ae heart !

'Twas then we sat on ae laigh bink,
  To leir ilk ither lear ;
And tones, and looks, and smiles were shed,
  Remembered evermair.

I wonder, Jeanie, aften yet,
  When sitting on that bink,
Cheek touchin' cheek, loof lock'd in loof,
  What our wee heads could think !
When baith bent doun ower ae braid page
  Wi' ae buik on our knee,
Thy lips were on thy lesson, but
  My lesson was in thee.

Oh, mind ye how we hung our heads,
  How cheeks brent red wi' shame,
Whene'er the schule-weans laughin' said,
  We cleek'd thegither hame ?
And mind ye o' the Saturdays
  (The schule then skail't at noon),
When we ran aff to speel the braes—
  The broomy braes o' June :

My head rins round and round about,
  My heart flows like a sea,
As ane by ane the thochts rush back
  O' schule-time and o' thee.
O mornin' life ! O mornin' luve !
  O lichtsome days and lang,
When hinnied hopes around our hearts,
  Like simmer blossoms sprang !

Oh, mind ye, luve, how aft we left
　The deavin' dinsome toun,
To wander by the green burnside,
　And hear its water croon ?
The simmer leaves hung ower our heads,
　The flowers burst round our feet,
And in the gloaming o' the wud
　The throssil whusslit sweet.

The throssil whusslit in the wud,
　The burn sung to the trees,
And we, with nature's heart in tune,
　Concerted harmonies ;
And on the knowe abune the burn
　For hours thegither sat
In the silentness o' joy, till baith
　Wi' very gladness grat.

Aye, aye, dear Jeanie Morrison,
　Tears trinkled down your cheek,
Like dew-beads on a rose, yet nane
　Had ony power to speak !
That was a time, a blessed time,
　When hearts were fresh and young,
When freely gush'd all feelings forth,
　Unsyllabled—unsung !

I marvel, Jeanie Morrison,
　Gin I hae been to thee
As closely twined wi' earliest thochts
　As ye hae been to me ?

Oh, tell me gin their music fills
   Thine ear as it does mine;
Oh, say gin e'er your heart grows grit
   Wi' dreamings o' langsyne!

I've wander'd east, I've wander'd west,
   I've borne a weary lot;
But in my wanderings far or near
   Ye never were forgot.
The fount that first burst frae this heart
   Still travels on its way,
And channels deeper as it rins,
   The life of luve's young day.

O dear, dear Jeanie Morrison,
   Since we were sinder'd young,
I've never seen your face, nor heard
   The music o' your tongue;
But I could hug all wretchedness,
   And happy could I dee,
Did I but ken your heart still dream'd
   O' bygane days and me!

             WILLIAM MOTHERWELL.

OF A' THE AIRTS THE WIND CAN BLAW.

OF a' the airts the wind can blaw,
  I dearly like the west,
For there the bonnie lassie lives,
  The lassie I lo'e best :
The wild woods grow, and rivers row,
  And mony a hill between ;
But day and night my fancy's flight
  Is ever wi' my Jean.

I see her in the dewy flowers,
  I see her sweet and fair ;
I hear her in the tunefu' birds,
  I hear her charm the air :
There's not a bonnie flower that springs
  By fountain, shaw, or green,
There's not a bonnie bird that sings,
  But minds me o' my Jean.

BURNS.

MAY-MORN SONG.

THE grass is wet with shining dews,
   Their silver bells hang on each tree;
While opening flower and bursting bud
   Breathe incense forth unceasingly:
The mavis pipes in greenwood shaw,
   The throstle glads the spreading thorn,
And cheerily the blythesome lark
   Salutes the rosy face of morn.
      'Tis early prime;
        And hark, hark, hark,
      His merry chime
        Chirrups the lark.
Chirrup, chirrup! he heralds in
The jolly sun with matin hymn.

Come, come, my love, and May-dews shake
   In pailfuls from each drooping bough,
They'll give fresh lustre to the bloom
   That breaks upon thy young cheek now.
O'er hill and dale, o'er waste and wood,
   Aurora's smiles are streaming free;

With earth it seems brave holiday,
  In heaven it looks high jubilee:
     And it is right;
      For mark, love, mark,
     How, bathed in light,
      Chirrups the lark.
Chirrup, chirrup! he upward flies,
Like holy thoughts to cloudless skies.

They lack all heart who cannot feel
  The voice of heaven within them thrill
In summer morn, when, mounting high
  This merry minstrel sings his fill.
Now let us seek yon bosky dell,
  Where brightest wildflowers choose to be,
And where its clear stream murmurs on,
  Meet type of our love's purity.
     No witness there;
      And o'er us, hark,
     High in the air
      Chirrups the lark.
Chirrup, chirrup! away soars he,
Bearing to heaven my vows to thee.
             MOTHERWELL.

MY AIN COUNTRIE.

THE sun rises bright in France,
  And fair sets he;
But he has tint the blythe blink he had
  In my ain countrie.
Oh, gladness comes to many
  But sorrow comes to me,
As I look o'er the wide ocean
  To my ain countrie.

Oh, it's not my ain ruin
  That saddens aye my e'e,
But the love I left in Galloway
  Wi' bonnie bairnies three;
My hamely hearth burnt bonnie,
  And smiled my fair Marie:
I've left my heart behind me
  In my ain countrie.

The bud comes back to summer,
    And the blossom to the tree;
But I win back—oh, never,
    To my ain countrie.
I'm leal to the high Heaven,
    Which will be leal to me;
And there I'll meet ye a' sune
    Frae my ain countrie.

ALLAN CUNNINGHAM.

DINNA FORGET.

DINNA forget, laddie, dinna forget,
Mak' me not wish that we never had met,
Wide though we sever;
Parted for ever,
Willie, when far awa', dinna forget.

When the star of the gloaming is shining above,
Think how aft it hath lighted the tryst of our love,
And deem it an angel's e'e heaven hath set
To watch thee, to warn thee,
Then dinna forget.

ANON.

THE AULD MAN.

BUT lately seen in gladsome green,
　　The woods rejoiced the day,
　Through gentle showers the laughing flowers
　　In double pride were gay;
　But now our joys are fled
　　On winter blasts awa';
　Yet maiden May, in rich array,
　　Again shall bring them a'.

　But my white pow nae kindly thowe
　　Shall melt the snaws of age;
　My trunk of eild, but buss or beild,
　　Sinks in time's wintry rage.
　Oh, age has weary days,
　　And nights o' sleepless pain!
　Thou golden time o' youthful prime,
　　Why com'st thou not again?

BURNS.

ADIEU FOR EVERMORE.

IT was a' for our richtfu' king
    We left fair Scotland's strand;
It was a' for our richtfu' king
    We e'er saw Irish land, my dear,
      We e'er saw Irish land.

Now a' is done that man can do,
    And a' is done in vain:
My love, my native land, farewell;
    For I maun cross the main, my dear,
      For I maun cross the main.

He turn'd him richt and round about
    Upon the Irish shore,
And ga'e his bridle-reins a shake,
    With, adieu for evermore, my love,
      With, adieu for evermore.

The sodger frae the war returns,
　The sailor frae the main ;
But I hae parted frae my love,
　Never to meet again, my love,
　　Never to meet again.

When day is gane, and nicht is come,
　And a' folk bound to sleep,
I think on him that's far awa'
　The lee-lang night, and weep, my dear,
　　The lee-lang night, and weep.

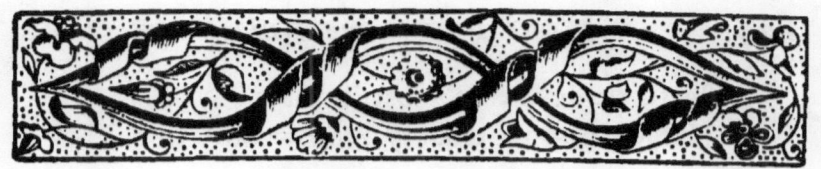

FORGET-ME-NOT.

FORGET thee, love?—no, not whilst heaven
　　Spans its starred vault across the sky;
　Oh, may I never be forgiven,
　　If e'er I cause that heart a sigh!
Sooner shall the forget-me-not
　　Shun the fringed brook by which it grows,
And pine for some sequestered spot,
　　Where not a silver ripple flows.
By the blue heaven that bends above me,
Dearly and fondly do I love thee!

They fabled not in days of old
　　That love neglected soon will perish,—
Throughout all time the truth doth hold
　　That what we love we ever cherish.
For when the sun neglects the flower,
　　And the sweet pearly dews forsake it,
It hangs its head, and from that hour
　　Prays only unto death to take it.
So may I droop, by all above me,
If once this heart doth cease to love thee!

The turtle-dove that's lost its mate,
  Hides in some gloomy greenwood shade,
And there alone mourns o'er its fate,
  With plumes for ever disarrayed :
Alone! alone! it there sits cooing :—
  Deem'st thou, my love, what it doth seek?
'Tis death the mournful bird is wooing,
  In murmurs through its plaintive beak.
So will I mourn, by all above me,
If in this world I cease to love thee!

———◆———

THE SHEPHERD TO THE FLOWERS.

SWEET violets, love's paradise, that spread
Your gracious odours, which you, couched, bear
  Within your paly faces,
Upon the gentle wing of some calm-breathing wind,
  That plays amidst the plain!
  If, by the favour of propitious stars, you gain,
Such grace as in my Lady's bosom place to find,
  Be proud to touch those places :
And when her warmth your moisture forth doth wear,
  Whereby her dainty parts are sweetly fed,
You, honours of the flowery meads, I pray,
  You pretty daughters of the earth and sun,
With mild and seemly breathing straight display
  My bitter sighs that have my heart undone!

RALEIGH.

SWEET DAY, SO COOL.

WEET day, so cool, so calm, so bright,
    The bridal of the earth and sky,
Sweet dews shall weep thy fall to-night,
          For thou must die.

Sweet rose, whose hue, angry and brave,
    Bids the rash gazer wipe his eye,
Thy root is ever in its grave,—
          And thou must die.

Sweet spring, full of sweet days and roses,
    A box where sweets compacted lie;
My music shews you have your closes,—
          And all must die.

Only a sweet and virtuous soul,
    Like season'd timber, never gives,
But when the whole world turns to coal,
          Then chiefly lives.
                GEORGE HERBERT.

THAT SONG AGAIN!

THAT song again! its wailing strain
   Brings back the thoughts of other hours,—
The forms I ne'er may see again,—
   And brightens all life's faded flowers.

In mournful murmurs o'er mine ear
   Remember'd echoes seem to roll,
And sounds I never more can hear
   Make music in my lonely soul.

That swell again!—now full and high
   The tide of feeling flows along,
And many a thought that claims a sigh
   Seems mingling with the magic song.

The forms I loved—and loved in vain,
   The hopes I nursed—to see them die,
With fleetness, brightness, through my brain
   In phantom beauty wander by.

Then touch the lyre, my own dear love!
  My soul is like a troubled sea,
And turns from all below, above,
  In fondness, to the harp and thee !
T. K. HERVEY.

CUPID AND THE DIAL.

One day young frolic Cupid tried
  To scatter roses o'er the hours,
And on the dial's face to hide
  The course of time with many flowers.

By chance his rosy wreaths had wound
  Upon the hands and forced them on ;
And when he look'd again he found
  The hours had pass'd—the time was gone.

" Alas," said Love, and dropp'd his flowers,
  " I've lost my time in idle play ;
The sweeter I would make the hours,
  The quicker they are pass'd away."
ANON.

"SERVANT TO A WOODEN CRADLE."

OME, visit the flowers, thy cousins,
God's dear little lamb, and mine !
See where, lit by one flaming crystal,
The gems of the greenhouse shine !
The leaves of this rose thou shalt scatter
With the strength of thy infant will ;
Thou hast ravished the form of the flower,
See ! the heart keeps its sweetness still.

The flowers have a dark, sad mother,
Whose bosom is bare to view ;
So they haste, in their springtide beauty,
To clothe her own heart anew.
They perish ; but she endureth,
To faint in the Winter's scorn,
With a life-warmth buried within her
Through which other Springs are born.

As the shadows dance hither and thi.her,
The gleams of thy consciousness pass,
As a lamp wakes its fitful glimmer
In the heart of a sleeping glass.

The shrouded ghost of the future
Stands near, while I hold thee fast;
And the traits of my race turn slowly
My thoughts to the long-linked past.

O Future! what sorrows gather
In the folds of thy hanging veil?
O Past, shalt thou flower further
In passions comprest and pale!
O thou who art past and future,
Thou Present of life and soul!
We lift our sad eyes to thy features,
Our thoughts to thy great control.

Thy manhood lies crouching within thee,
For the leap of its coming years;
Thy heart takes its long vibration
From the mother's fountain of tears;
The helpful things and the hurtful
Weave round thee their waiting spell:
Oh! look to the God that commands them,
And all shall be suffered well.

JULIA W. HOWE.

FLOWERS IN A GARDEN.

THE rose like a nymph to the bath addrest,
Which unveiled the depth of her glowing breast,
Till, fold after fold, to the fainting air
The soul of her beauty and love lay bare;

And the wand-like lily, which lifted up,
As a Mænad, its moonlight-coloured cup,
Till the fiery star, which is its eye,
Gazed through the clear dew on the tender sky;

And the jessamine faint, and the sweet tuberose,
The sweetest flower for scent that blows;
And all rare blossoms from every clime
Grew in that garden in perfect prime;

And on the stream whose inconstant bosom
Was prankt, under boughs of embowering blossom,
With golden and green light, slanting through
Their heaven of many a tangled hue,

Broad water-lilies lay tremulously,
And starry river-buds glimmered by,
And around them the soft stream did glide and dance
With a motion of sweet sound and radiance.

And the sinuous paths of lawn and of moss,
Which led through the garden along and across,
Some open at once to the sun and the breeze,
Some lost among bowers of blossoming trees,

Were all paved with daisies and delicate bells,
As fair as the fabulous asphodels,
And flowerets which drooping as day drooped too,
Fell into pavilions, white, purple, and blue,
To roof the glow-worm from the evening dew.

And from this undefiled Paradise
The flowers (as an infant's awakening eyes
Smile on its mother, whose singing sweet
Can first lull, and at last must awaken it),

When heaven's blithe winds had unfolded them,
As mine-lamps enkindle a hidden gem,
Shone smiling to heaven, and every one
Shared joy in the light of the gentle sun.

SHELLEY.

REMEMBRANCE.

HERE was a time when thy dear face to me
Was but a dream, with nameless pangs between.
Three happy years upheld the fatal screen
Whose fall left blank and bitterness for thee.

As one who at a gracious drama sits,
And builds long vistas in its magic ways,
" For this must come, and this;" and while he stays
The end consigns him to the silent streets :

So did I stand when thy sweet play was done,
Wondering what spell the curtain still should hide,
Waiting and weeping, till my saintly guide
Took by the hand, and pitying said, " Pass on."

So thou art hid again, and wilt not come
For any knocking at the veilèd door :
Nor mother-pangs, nor nature, can restore
The heart's delight and blossom of thy home.

And I with others, in the outer court,
Must sadly follow the excluding will,
In painful admiration of the skill
Of God, who speaks his sweetest sentence short.
JULIA W. HOWE (*an American authoress*).